ONE, TWO, THREE . . . TOGETHER

Other books by Jocelyn Saint James:

Romancing the King

ONE, TWO, THREE ... TOGETHER

•

Jocelyn Saint James

AVALON BOOKS
NEW YORK

Published by Thomas Bouregy & Co., Inc.
160 Madison Avenue, New York, NY 10016

Library of Congress Cataloging-in-Publication Data

Saint James, Jocelyn.
    One, two, three— together / Jocelyn Saint James.
        p. cm.
    ISBN 978-0-8034-7762-9 (acid-free paper)   1. Mothers and
daughters—Fiction.   2. Dance schools—Fiction.   3. Dance—
Competitions—Fiction.   I. Title.
    PS3619.A398O54 2010
    813'.6—dc22
                                                              2009054252

PRINTED IN THE UNITED STATES OF AMERICA
ON ACID-FREE PAPER
BY HADDON CRAFTSMEN, BLOOMSBURG, PENNSYLVANIA

This book is dedicated to the loving memory of Jocelyn Saint James.

Words cannot express the joy she brought into my life and the sorrow I feel now that she is gone. Jude, you were the best sister in the whole world. —*Love, Beth*

Chapter One

Turn, bend, glide, dip—
Move light as a feather.
Toe, heel, point, twist—
Step one, two, three . . . together.

"Are we having fun yet?" Liz Pruitt gazed over the crowd of revelers from the pavilion in Olson Town Park, drips from the sweating glass of cold lemonade in her hand splashing onto the callused toes that protruded from her strappy sandals. She turned to her best friend, Julie Baines, wondering why the usually talkative woman had yet to reply.

Julie's tongue shot from her mouth, chameleonlike, licking her ice cream cone with a quick swirl. "I'm

1

having fun." She gulped. "Thought you always liked Ontario Fest. It's *the* big event of the year in Olson."

Liz sighed. "I did. I mean, I do. It's just . . ."

"Different?" Julie finished Liz's sentence and took another lick of her cone, catching the drips.

"Yeah, different." Liz dragged a mouthful of lemonade through the straw, draining the liquid from the glass with a long, sucking sound. "We haven't missed an Ontario Fest since high school. Wouldn't be the end of June without it, right?"

Julie munched on the cone, brushing off the crumbs that fell onto her blouse. "I know I'm a slob," she said just as Liz opened her mouth to say those same words. Fifteen years of being best friends had given them the knack for finishing each other's thoughts.

Liz sighed and gestured with a sweep of her arm. "This, all of this, just seems so *different* from Syracuse." She dragged again on the straw, vacuuming up the ice cubes melting rapidly from the heat.

Julie popped the last of the cone into her mouth and rearranged the points of her pixie-blond hair onto her cheeks, making her look like every doll Liz remembered having as a child. "Well, in case you haven't noticed, Olson *is* a bit different from Syracuse," she said sarcastically. "Only about a trillion fewer people here. And no building over three stories high. And when's the last time you saw a clown making balloon animals on Salina Street?" She nodded toward the clown surrounded by giggling children. "At least not one hired to be there!"

Liz leaned against the waist-high railing and looked at the festival crowd. "I like it here. It's home."

"But you live in Syracuse."

"That's just it. I live in Syracuse, but Olson is my home. Sure, Olson is tiny and fairly uneventful, but it's hard not to love the Lake Ontario shore. As much as I complain about coming back to help Mom with her dance recital every year, it's always good to have an excuse to return."

"Why do you need an excuse?" Julie pulled a bag of peanuts from her purse. "Syracuse is only a few hours away. Just come back, you know, to come back."

Liz smirked. "Are you forgetting who my mother is?" She thrust back her head and closed her eyes. The warm sun penetrated her neck and shoulders, massaging her tense muscles. The sun prickled her cheeks, and she imagined the red tint rising on her fair complexion, accompanied by her mother's warnings to stay out of the damaging rays.

Liz shot her head upright when she heard the dramatic flare-up of the band and the excited howl of dancers stampeding the makeshift dance floor. Any festival-goers in earshot of the band joined in an enthusiastic clapping to "Rocky Top," accompanied by hoots, singing, and bobbing heads. The old song had become a festival favorite and, as tradition had it, would be played at least a dozen times throughout the weekend event.

Liz and Julie joined the clapping, then locked arms

and did a quick spin. They laughed and gawked at the dancers who had morphed into a playful frenzy.

"*They're* sure having fun." Liz bounced her head to the beat. When one dancer in particular caught her attention, she blinked a few times to clear her vision, then steadied her head to maintain her focus.

"Why aren't you out there on that dance floor, Twinkletoes?" Julie snapped her fingers to the tune. "Never knew you to resist a dance."

Liz didn't answer; she didn't even hear her friend. Her eyes were still riveted on the dance floor.

"Hey." Julie elbowed her.

Liz shook her head, a lurch back to reality as she looked toward Julie. "Say something?" Her eyes drifted back to the dance floor. She couldn't look away. Wouldn't.

"What could possibly be more interesting than what I have to say?" Julie mocked, turning her head to follow her friend's line of vision. "Ooohh," she murmured when she latched on to the target.

"Who's that?" Liz didn't need to point out the person she was referring to in the sea of dancers.

In the middle of the floor, swerving, twirling, and dipping to each note, spinning any woman who came within reach of his muscular arms, was a man whose abdomen rippled beneath a formfitting red T-shirt. Even from where she stood, Liz could see the pronounced dimples in his tanned cheeks and the sun glistening on his blond hair. He wore sunglasses, but she knew, just knew, his eyes were blue. Crystal blue. His type always had eyes like that.

Even if Liz hadn't been a dancer herself, the vision of this man with the movie-star charm and supermodel good looks would have been enough to keep her attention. But his dance moves and the way his body flowed seamlessly with the music commanded much more than an intrigued glance and admiration for all things beautiful. She hadn't seen such spirited, talented dance moves since . . . she couldn't even remember. College, maybe? Her internship with the William Dance Company in New York? Perhaps, but certainly never in Olson. Talent aside, she hadn't seen such a handsome man dance with so much style and confidence since—well, never.

"So he *is* back in town," said Julie, a broad, devilish smile accompanying her words.

"Who's back?" Liz's eyes were still locked on the dancer, mesmerized by more than just an entertaining performance.

"Tyler. Tyler Augustine."

Liz tore her eyes from the dance floor and snapped her head toward Julie, wrinkling her brow. "That's Tyler Augustine? From high school?"

"The one and only. Who could forget the quarterback, track star, prom king, straight-A student, lead in the senior play? Best catch in the school, according to any girl with a pulse."

Liz returned her attention to Tyler. Was that really

him? When he turned his back, she saw the broad shoulders and the hair curled ever so slightly over his collar. Sighting confirmed. It was the same view she'd enjoyed for four years of homeroom. She willed him to turn around and notice her.

"So it is Tyler." She was unable to suppress a smile. *Settle down,* she warned herself. Almost twelve years had passed since she'd seen that view, and still she recalled the broad shoulders, smooth neck, and fashionably disheveled hair. "If I remember, Tyler was quite, shall we say, mischievous." She raised her eyebrows.

Julie smiled broadly. "That's putting it mildly. Sometimes I wondered if trouble was attracted to him like a magnet. Who cares? All part of his bottomless pit of charm."

"I remember the day he drove his Corvette across the front lawn of the school and tore up the new shrubs. I don't know how charming that was."

Julie nodded, a goofy grin covering her face. "That was very cool. Like something out of some old James Dean movie."

Liz opened her mouth in shock. "Very cool? Very stupid, if you ask me. How could someone be so careless? The rumor was, his father took away the Corvette and made him replant all the shrubs—by hand. Then Tyler had to mow the principal's lawn for the rest of the summer and repaint the lines on the tennis court. He really got into trouble that time."

Julie shoved a few peanuts into her mouth. "So, he had a little wild streak. I'm sure he's outgrown that."

Liz turned back to watch Tyler jump, spin, and then dip one of the girls who had crowded around him, all with a perfectly natural rhythm. Judging from those moves, it sure didn't look as if he'd outgrown his wild streak—or even tamed it much. Even if he wasn't taking out shrubbery any longer, she'd bet the mischievous Tyler from high school hadn't changed much over the years.

Liz smiled, wondering if the man before her could overshadow the mythical teenage boy she remembered. That same bad-boy style she remembered distinctly and had innocently fantasized about hoisted red flags in her brain while it sent shivers down her spine all these years later. Her mother's voice, warning the teenage Liz to stay away from boys like that, resounded louder than ever in her head. She wanted to yell out, "Quiet, Grace. I'm not a kid anymore." And, apparently, neither was Tyler.

The music stopped, the crowd gave one last rousing hoot, and the dancers tumbled from the floor, laughing and wiggling to the rhythm lingering in their heads. As Liz had always believed, the sign of a good dance was the feeling that remained after the music stopped.

"That was fun," said Julie, still snapping her fingers.

"Sure was." Liz stretched to see the whereabouts of Tyler Augustine as he melted into the crowd and then disappeared from view. Like the fog that burned off the lakeshore as the sun rose, signaling a new day, a new beginning, Tyler had evaporated. As it should be—with this and with all memories. Once they've served their purpose, all good things should disappear without fanfare. Liz wasn't interested in keeping the past alive.

When Liz had come to town three days previously to help her mother with the dance recital, she had been prepared—and resigned—to spend four crazy days surrounded by overly excited children who were frantic about ill-fitting costumes and forgotten dance steps. And she hadn't been disappointed. As always, her mother flitted around the high school auditorium, doling out stern but compassionate last-minute advice, absorbing the pandemonium as if it were the air she breathed, her life force. And it was just that.

"This is more than merely a dance recital," Grace had said to her students a million times during the rehearsal and the show. "Dancing is life. Feel the beauty. Feel the passion."

Liz wasn't sure if the three-year-olds in bumblebee costumes understood her mother's message, but she gave Grace credit for trying.

Liz knew that Grace took her own words to heart. Dance was everything to her. As she'd done since she was five years old, Liz watched in awe as her mother performed a ballet number in the recital, the special number reserved for the dance teacher, the model of what the dancers could aspire to someday be. As she stood tall and statuesque *en pointe,* her mother's graceful limbs moved effortlessly to the music until she, the music, and the dance were indistinguishable from one another. One perfect, breathtaking entity cultivated from years of study and dedication. A lifetime of extraordinary moments that had become insignificant except for this particular instant.

As usual, when Grace's dance ended, the crowd, packed tightly in the auditorium, stood and cheered, and she smiled and glowed, a genuine happiness and inner peace Liz saw for only those few minutes each year. A happiness fueled not as much by that dance but by the memory of her days as a prima ballerina.

Now that the previous day's recital was over, Liz was prepared to plant that experience in the archives, as she'd planted her memory of Tyler many years ago, and return to Syracuse. Back to her dog-grooming business, back to her life. Unlike her mother, who chose to be defined by this one dance a year and the memories it conjured, Liz preferred to deal with the present instead of allowing the past to be her daily companion. She needed more, but she wasn't sure what *more* was.

"So long again, Tyler," she muttered, almost inaudibly, to no one.

"Huh?" asked Julie.

Liz cleared her throat. "Nothing. Just thinking out loud." She was glad her friend hadn't heard.

"Let's go look at the vendors," Julie suggested. "I hear there's a stand selling spices. I want to check those out for some new recipes I want to make for the restaurant.

What do you think of pork with a cinnamon-honey glaze? Maybe a touch of mint."

"You're the chef," Liz replied. "Have I ever spit out anything you made?"

Liz followed Julie through the thickening crowd and out of the pavilion. "I need a bottle of water. Want one?" She turned toward the stand decorated with a six-foot-tall cup of a nondescript, pink, foamy beverage and frowned at the long line.

"No thanks," replied Julie. "I'll go on without you so I can get over there before all the spices get snapped up. Meet you there."

Liz took her place at the end of the line and started digging in her purse for her money. She popped her sunglasses onto the top of her head for a clearer view into the cavern that doubled as a purse. She moved forward a couple of steps, her eyes focused on her purse, while she retrieved two quarters. With money in hand, she snapped her purse shut, repositioned her sunglasses on her face, and raised her head, ready for an agonizing wait in the sun that Grace would insist had turned her skin into leather.

When she turned her eyes forward, she caught her breath and was transported back fifteen years to her freshman homeroom. The neck, the hair, the unreachable aura that belonged to Tyler Augustine. In front of her. Just inches away. The storybook teenager turned close-enough-to-touch man.

Stunned, she let the quarters fall from her hand.

They rolled like little silver wheels until they came to rest against Tyler's brown leather deck shoes.

He bent to pick them up. Holding them in his outstretched hand, he turned to Liz. "Yours?"

She gulped and nodded, holding out her hand while he deposited the coins. "Thanks."

He smiled widely, the dimples looking deeper than Liz remembered. "Hold on to them. Money is at a premium these days. Every quarter counts." He winked a crystal blue eye, exactly the gemstone color Liz remembered, and turned around. Then he quickly turned back to Liz, looked at her curiously as if he was trying to see through her sunglasses, and smiled again. "Enjoy the festival." He turned and moved several steps ahead in line.

"You too," Liz said to the all-too-familiar back of his head. She scolded herself for reverting to her awkward high school self. Tyler was just a person, like everyone else, not the romanticized star he'd become in the minds of so many doe-eyed girls. She should strike up a conversation, re-introduce herself, talk about old times. What old times? The fact that she had just existed behind him for four years, largely unknown and unnoticed, hardly made for old times. They had traveled in different circles in high school, so they certainly didn't have that in common. They'd even lived in totally different parts of town. He was raised in that breathtaking Victorian mansion on Clover Hill, undoubtedly the most extravagant house in town. Legend told of a bowling alley in the basement, fireplaces in every bedroom, and closets as big as the school gymnasium.

She'd lived in the much more modest section by the lake known as The Flats in a house barely large enough for her mother and her. Two different people, two different worlds. But that was years ago. Wasn't time the great equalizer? Weren't they now just two people waiting in line for a cold drink on a scorching summer day? *Just talk to him.*

By the time Liz finished arguing with herself, Tyler was at the counter, placing his order. He bought a bottle of cola, looked again at Liz, nodded, then moved toward the crowd. Before becoming absorbed by the masses, he turned yet one more time to her, smiled widely, and tipped his bottle.

Liz returned his smile as she took her place at the counter. "A bottle of water," she said to the cashier, placing the runaway coins and a dollar on the counter. "Actually, make that two. I'm thirstier than I thought I was."

Chapter Two

Liz pulled her rusted Chevy Cavalier into the driveway of her mother's house, parking in front of the garage that had been converted into the Tiptoe Dance Studio when Liz was in kindergarten. Rex, her hyperactive border collie, stood at the chain-link fence, padding back and forth, barking with fervor, the black and white markings on his face making him look like a performing harlequin.

Before Liz had even turned off the engine, Mrs. Collins, the next door neighbor, was standing next to the car.

"Hi, Mrs. Collins." Liz smiled as she opened the door, forcing the pudgy-cheeked woman to back up a few steps.

The elderly woman twisted the bottom of her apron,

13

and her face melted with worry. "Liz, go right to the hospital. Your mother, she broke her leg. I called the ambulance about an hour ago."

"Oh, no! What happened?" Liz felt the blood drain from her head, and her knees weakened.

Mrs. Collins fanned herself with one hand, catching her breath as the words flew from her mouth. "She was walking down the steps into the backyard when your dog ran up to her and knocked her down. Good thing Grace is so flexible from all those years of dancing, or she could have been more seriously injured." Mrs. Collins ran a hand through her flyaway gray hair. "You must hurry to the hospital, Liz. Your mother is alone. She has no one else."

Guilt washed over Liz. While she'd been ogling Tyler Augustine and fantasizing about the back of his head, Rex was wiping out her mother. Grace would surely claim a conspiracy and demonize Rex, twisting this into such finely woven blame that Liz would be haunted by it for the rest of her life. A decade from now, as Liz was opening Christmas presents or blowing out the candles on her birthday cake or doing something that was supposed to evoke fun and family, her mother would be reminding her of "the time your dog tried to kill me."

Grace had always been one of those mothers who never had to raise her voice or rant and rave for Liz to behave. She was much too dignified, too refined. Just a well-practiced lift of a pencil-thin eyebrow or a whispered comment sharpened like a stiletto was enough to drive home the point. While the neighborhood mothers swatted their children with dish towels, screeched at them out of flapping screen doors, and threatened to ground them until they were twenty-one, Grace just calmly said, "Now, we know better than to do that, don't we, Liz?" And then she would walk away, leaving Liz to be mature and simply comply, no questions asked. Even when Liz upped the ante and did benign things like eat all the candy from the bowl Grace kept on her desk or wear Grace's jewelry without asking—anything she thought would get a rise from her mother—Grace calmly admonished Liz for her actions, turned her aquiline nose into the air, and walked away. Done deal. No need for the queen to say more.

Liz imagined her mother lying at the bottom of the steps, leg bent like a pretzel, and still not mustering the humility to yell out. It was a small miracle that Mrs. Collins had found her.

Liz jumped back into the car and sped out of the driveway, the tires squealing as she slammed on the brakes, threw the car into drive, and raced down the street. The hospital, only two miles away, seemed as distant as Mars, and she felt weighed down by the panic she fought to control. If anything happened to her mother, she would— what would she do?

Mrs. Collins was right—Grace had only Liz in her life. Liz's father had died in a construction accident when she was four. Her father's parents lived in Phoenix. Although she shared phone calls and cards with them

throughout the years, she rarely saw them. Her grand-
mother and Grace never quite saw eye to eye, and the
rift had widened after Liz's father died and Grace re-
fused their offer to move her and Liz to Phoenix. Her
mother's parents had died before Liz was born. Grace
had only one brother—a college professor who lived in
Florida—and they had only infrequent contact with
him.

So today, at this moment of fear and uncertainty, Liz
and Grace were once again alone, something that made
her sad—and resentful.

"Why am I all she has?" Liz asked aloud as she
drove too quickly, clenching the steering wheel, barely
slowing down at the stop signs. "Did I ask her to avoid
any meaningful relationship with other men? Did I ask
her to be so impossible that, despite her beauty, intelli-
gence, and talent, men couldn't stand her? Come on,
Grace. Do you have any idea how many men would
have jumped at the chance to marry a former ballerina
from the New York City Ballet?" Her voice grew in vol-
ume and anger as the unanswered questions escaped
her lips, filling the void in the car.

Her private tirade ceased when, in the rearview mirror, she saw a motorcycle speed up behind and hover
on her bumper. She was driving well above the speed
limit, so she could only guess how fast that guy was going. Liz's first impulse was to beep the horn and motion
for the speeder to back off. Her scowl turned into up-
raised eyebrows when she took a second look. She'd

recognize those dimples anywhere, even at fifty miles an hour. Tyler. He was either in a hurry to go somewhere, or he was a reckless driver for the fun of it. She guessed the second possibility was the right one.

Tyler turned left at the next intersection, just before Liz turned into the hospital parking lot. "Sure, just keep going. Enjoy your little ride while my life falls apart," she whined aloud. "Don't slow down on my account. After all, I'm just Liz Pruitt."

"It's terrible, Liz, just terrible," Grace moaned from her hospital bed. Her heavily casted leg hung in traction, and she slipped a bony white hand from under the blanket and lifted it, elegantly poised, toward Liz.

Liz took her hand, noting how thin and cold it felt. She couldn't remember the last time she'd held her mother's hand. "It's not that bad, Mom." Liz was unsure of how to comfort her. "The doctor said you have two breaks, but they're clean breaks. So they'll heal in no time." Liz forced a smile.

"I doubt that," said Grace weakly, turning her head away.

"Since when are you a doctor?" Liz tried to inject some levity into her voice, but she wasn't so sure her frustration didn't show. "You're going to be fine."

Grace turned back to Liz, staring with piercing green eyes. " 'Fine' for a normal person. Not 'fine' for a dancer." Grace swallowed hard. "Especially not 'fine' for a ballerina."

Liz sighed. "Mom, don't be so dramatic." She wished she could retract those words. Telling her mother not to be dramatic was as useless as asking her to cut off her head.

Grace's jaw squared, and her eyes flashed with anger. She tightened her grip on Liz's hand, yet her voice remained soft. "Well, a leg that has danced in the greatest ballets on the finest stages in the country has just been destroyed. Once the bone heals, arthritis will set in. My perfectly symmetrical posture will be compromised; then my back will weaken. Soon I'll become totally disabled. Depression will follow, and then . . ." She sighed loudly. "And then it will be just a matter of time."

Liz rolled her eyes upward, recalling her mother's performance in *Swan Lake* thirteen years before in the Olson Community Theater. At that time, Grace had been equally dramatic about the seriousness of the story and the appalling amateur ballet skills of the others in the cast. " 'Matter of time' for what, Mom?"

Grace's expression softened. "For me to be . . . gone. For you to be . . . alone."

"Oh, Mom, please. You're not going anywhere—and I won't be alone. Just you wait, before you know it, your leg will be fine. By the time your autumn classes roll around, you'll be *chasse*-ing like there's no tomorrow." Liz reached over and pushed back a strand of jet black hair from her mother's forehead, causing Grace to flinch before she barely raised the corners of her mouth.

"And what about my summer classes? They start next week."

Liz pulled the chair close to the bed. "Cancel them. The people in Olson can survive without their dance lessons for a summer."

Grace slumped lower into the bed, her pale complexion fading into the white sheets, rendering her almost invisible. Maybe she *was* going—somewhere. A shiver of panic tingled through Liz.

"Perhaps they can, but I can't," said Grace.

Liz smiled, touched by her mother's dedication to her students. Maybe there was a side of her Liz hadn't seen. "The students really mean a lot to you, don't they, Mom?"

Grace looked at Liz with eyes sunken more deeply than usual, eyeliner still intact and jutting from the outer corners like thorns. "Of course they do. But I also need the money. There are bills to pay."

The practical Grace was alive and well, obliterating the emotional Grace. That was more like it. All was almost normal again, and Liz felt the shiver fade.

"Can't you just use savings for a couple of months?"

Grace cracked a thin smile. "Savings? What savings, you silly girl? The dance business isn't so lucrative that it would afford a single woman, one solely responsible for herself, to have a savings account. After the usual payments are made, there's little to go around. You must recall that after I provided for you, took care of the house, and kept the studio in business, there wasn't much left over."

Liz held her breath, the panic returning with intensity. She recalled the many times Grace had fumbled through her checkbook, trying to find out why the account wouldn't balance. And rummaging through drawers for the money she thought she had hidden. Grace had always made sure that Liz never lacked for anything, but money management and Grace had never gone hand in hand. "What about the home equity loan you took out last month for the new roof and windows? Will you have to start paying that back?" She stood, bracing herself for the answer.

Grace's nose twitched. "I . . . I'd forgotten about that. Yes, yes, I imagine that payment will also be due. Plus the loan I had to take out for the new studio floor."

Liz let her mother's hand drop, and she paced to the window. She strummed her chin and stared out onto Bridge Street, the town's main drag. She heard Grace whimper and turned to see a tear run down her face. The first tear she'd seen her mother shed since her father's death almost twenty-five years before.

"Don't worry, Mom. We'll think of something." She inhaled deeply, the scent of hospital disinfectant and medicine permeating her nose, almost causing her to gag. "I'm home."

Grace had eaten a light dinner, whined some more about her inevitable demise, complained about the nursing care, and then, thankfully, fell asleep. As soon as Grace's eyes shut, Liz hurried outside the hospital and sat on the bench by the main entrance to catch the waning sun and to wind down from the hectic day. She needed to pull herself together and collect her thoughts. And hope for a miracle.

She stared blankly at the street, watching cars whizz by and people enjoying a stroll on a warm evening. Maybe it was her mood or her imagination, but everyone seemed to be having fun except for her. Life was passing by, the world turning, while she felt perfectly miserable. She scolded herself for the self-pity, reminding herself that sometime within the next century her fun was sure to happen.

"There you are." Julie plopped onto the bench, causing Liz to jump.

"You scared me."

Julie sat back and crossed her legs, red Capri pants riding up and revealing a tattoo of tiny spatulas, pots, forks, and other cooking utensils encircling her ankle. "I yelled hi when I got out of the car, but you were in la-la land. When I stopped by your house, Mrs. Collins told me what happened. How's your mom?"

Liz slouched and moved her head in slow circles, stretching her neck muscles. "A couple of breaks in her leg, but she's acting like she has rabies or typhoid."

"Well, she is a dancer." Julie held up a bouquet of pink carnations. "For Grace." She sniffed the flowers with an exaggerated inhale. "Did you once say pink is her favorite color?"

"No, black is her favorite," said Liz, sarcasm not

totally false. "But she's going to love the flowers." Liz smiled. "You're a doll, even to the spider woman."

"Well, I've known your mom as long as I've known you, more than fifteen years." She started to laugh, covering her mouth with one hand. "Remember that day in high school when I first went to your house, and we were goofing around in your mom's dance studio? I got my shoelace tangled around the ballet barre and was hanging upside down. You and Grace had to cut me loose. She wasn't happy!"

"Girls, the ballet barre is *not* a toy!" Liz mocked, pinching together her lips, sucking in her cheeks, batting her eyelashes, and slicking back her bangs to mimic her mother. Liz and Julie leaned on each other, overtaken by fits of laughter.

"You're terrible!" Julie snorted.

"No, *she's* terrible!" laughed Liz.

"Oh, she is not." Julie wiped tears from the corners of her eyes. "Just a little . . . uptight."

Liz cleared her throat as the laughter subsided. "That's our Gracie."

"Give her credit. She's a fantastic dancer. Even at fifty-five she has the body of a ballerina and can hold her own with the best of them. Wish my legs were half as long."

Liz nodded. "I'll give her that much—she is beautiful and talented."

"You look like her, you know." Julie smirked.

"Do not!" Liz was adamant. She couldn't look like

her mother. Could she? Her mother was tall, slim, lithe. Liz was tall but fuller, broad-shouldered, and curvy. Grace's straight hair shone like ebony on fire. Liz's hair was blackish-brown yet indistinct and loosely curled, easily disheveled, and prone to frizzing. Her brown eyes were wide and round, unlike her mother's catlike emerald eyes. They both shared the same fair complexion, but Liz's had acquired a few freckles from the sun, something Grace detested.

"Yes, you do," Julie persisted. "Sure, there are some traits from your father probably, but you're like her, no doubt. You move just like her. Dance just like her."

Liz cocked her head at Julie, eyes opening wide with disbelief. Grace moved like a goddess. Effortless elegance. She floated with movements so silent and precise, she seemed to appear in a room like an apparition, not a person. Liz had always thought that her mother's name had predestined her beauty. Grace— she was that and more. Liz could never be so lovely, so striking.

"I dance like her?" Liz was still disbelieving of Julie's proclamation.

"Your mom is a ballerina, and you're more of a jazz and tap kind of girl, but there's no mistaking the classic Pruitt style." Julie poked Liz. "Grace isn't the only one who gets standing ovations at the recitals."

"The audience is just being nice because I'm her daughter." Liz brushed off her friend's comment with a flick of her hand.

"Wrong again. When are you going to give yourself a little credit?"

Liz shrugged as Julie's words seeped in. Maybe there were similarities. But she and her mother, alike? Not likely.

"Well, maybe Mom is a wonderful dancer and a beautiful woman, but she's a lousy bookkeeper. She won't be able to dance for a few months, but she's so in debt, she can't afford to close the studio while her leg heals." She rubbed her forehead and moaned.

Julie's amber-flecked eyes flew open, and she sat up straighter. "I always thought the dance studio was a good moneymaker. Grace seems to have a lot of students."

"Well, she must spend more than she takes in. She just had a new floor put in in the studio. I know that cost a small fortune. And she travels all over the country for seminars to keep up with her dancing."

Julie huffed. "She should be *giving* the seminars. People would pay to learn from a prima ballerina."

"I think she just likes being in the company of other professional dancers," Liz replied with resignation. "You know how it is, always drawn back to your own kind."

"What are you going to do?" asked Julie.

Liz shrugged and opened her palms upward. "What choice do I have? I'll have to stay here and run the studio for her."

"What about your job at the dog-grooming shop? Your apartment? Your life in Syracuse?"

"I'll take a leave from the shop and give up the apartment for now. Mr. Sarraino lets me rent month to month, so there's no lease to worry about. If it's still available when I'm ready to move back, I'll rent it again. If not, I'll be a homeless bum, eat out of Dumpsters, and push around my meager belongings in a shopping cart."

The women sat in silence as the enormity of Liz's impending situation sank in. What was she saying? Sure, she could easily run the dance studio, but she'd also have to take care of her mother. That challenge would far surpass a roomful of clumsy eight-year-olds trying to do a shuffle-ball-change.

"At least you'll finally get some use out of all your dance training. Your mom will be happy about that." Julie's tone was upbeat.

"I'm sure she will." Liz's voice dripped with cynicism. "I'm *sure* she will." Liz stood. "Let's go up to Mom's room before visiting hours end."

As they turned to enter the hospital, they were startled by the rip of a motorcycle stopping at the crosswalk in front of the hospital. Liz looked up, directly into a helmeted head sporting the unmistakable fringe of blond hair at the neck. Tyler turned and glanced her way, their eyes locking for a second. He smiled, and those cavernous dimples looked so deep, she felt she could fall into them.

He removed his goggles and winked at her. "The quarter lady!" he yelled, pointing a finger. Then he nodded slightly and left with an annoying roar of the engine.

"Was that . . . ?" asked Julie.

"Mr. Perfect himself," replied Liz. "None other than Tyler Augustine."

" 'Quarter lady'? Where was Tyler going in such a hurry?"

"Away," Liz sighed. "He's going away. And I'm staying."

Chapter Three

"Careful, Mom." Liz gently positioned her mother's casted leg in the passenger's seat of Grace's old but well-maintained Buick Park Avenue.

Grace moaned and sighed.

"What's wrong?" Liz opened the back door so Rex could jump in, then scooted around the car to take her place behind the wheel.

Grace wriggled until she found a comfortable position. "I don't know why you insisted on going for a drive. It's taken us twenty minutes just to get into the car." She pursed her lips. "This is not easy for a woman in my damaged condition."

Liz backed the car out of the driveway, being careful not to jostle it excessively and send thunderbolts into her mother's leg. "You're anything but damaged," she

27

said, shooting her mother a glance from the corner of her eye. "You've been home from the hospital for a week and haven't gone farther than the front porch. A ride will do you good." *And me too,* Liz refrained from adding. She'd been at her mother's beck and call for a week and was about to go crazy. They both needed some fresh air.

Rex, panting, popped his head into the front seat between Liz and Grace. His fur blew in the wind from the open window. Liz rubbed his ear.

"Did you have to bring *him*?" Grace pulled her head as far away from Rex as possible. "I don't like having a dog in my car."

"I'll vacuum the hair, and, yes, he needed to get out too." Liz scratched Rex's chin, causing him to lick her cheek.

"Just make sure he doesn't break my other leg," Grace sniped.

Liz offered no comment, deciding not to volley the first round. She turned the car onto Water Street, approaching the boat harbor. The July day was picture-perfect, ideal for spending on a boat or at least dreaming of being someplace other than cooped up in her mother's car.

Wishing wouldn't make it so.

The sun shimmered a brilliant yellow streak onto the lake, and waxen-looking seagulls bobbed in the gentle waves. A few wispy clouds painted the robin's egg blue sky with feathery streaks, and Liz wished she could throw a blanket onto a grassy patch, listen to the birds, and breathe the acrid-sweet lake air until night-fall. Olson at its finest.

"The harbor is certainly busy today. So many charter boats," Grace commented, for a moment distracted from her self-pity and snit about Rex. Fishing charters lined an entire side of the dock, signs advertising their serv-ices prominently displayed. "*Fishy Wishy,*" commented Grace as she read a sign on one boat and cracked a slight smile. "Amusing name."

"Look at that one: *A-lure-ing Adventure.*" Liz pointed to a red and white boat whose outriggers were in place, awaiting the next interested fisherman.

"Clever," Grace commented. "I like that." She turned to Liz and nodded. "Poetic in an obtuse, inane way."

Were Liz and her mother actually bonding over crazy boat names? Liz wouldn't complain. These were the first nonmedical words they'd exchanged since Grace broke her leg. Liz continued to drive slowly down the small road running parallel to the boardwalk and docks.

"So he *is* back." Grace pointed to a large white boat with a sea green wave pattern running across the side.

"That's a weird name," Liz commented.

"No, not a name," corrected Grace. "Over there on that charter called *Fish On.* That man. He's back in town."

Liz followed the point of her mother's slender finger straight to Tyler standing on the deck of *Fish On*, arms akimbo as he surveyed the surroundings. She slowed the car to a crawl and ducked down a bit behind the oversized steering wheel. She wasn't sure why she cared if Tyler saw her, but she did.

"Who's back in town?" Liz didn't want to mention her encounters with Tyler, insignificant as they were.

"The Augustine boy. Tyler." Grace turned slyly toward Liz. "You must remember him from high school."

Liz didn't respond.

"About a month ago, when I was visiting with Barbara Baker outside of church, Tyler's father, Sam, came by as he was leaving the service. He told Barbara that Tyler had returned a couple of months earlier to spend some time with his grandfather. The dear man was in his nineties and failing quickly. He hung on until Tyler showed up."

"So the grandfather died?" Liz tried to sound nonchalant and conversational instead of hungry for information.

"Yes, he did. I'm surprised Tyler is still in town. What could possibly keep him here now?" Grace shrugged and repositioned the silver barrette that secured her shoulder-length black hair behind her head.

Rex, in constant motion, paced in the backseat and popped his head out the window to bark at a squirrel scampering in the grass. Grace covered her ears and grimaced.

"Quiet, Rexie," said Liz. *Don't draw attention to us,* she wanted to add. The last thing she needed was for Tyler to see her. The dog continued yapping.

Tyler looked toward the car, studied Liz through the

open window, and then lifted his sunglasses for a better view. He broke into a wide grin that Liz interpreted to be a mix of surprise and mockery.

As she was reeling from Tyler's stare, Rex bolted through the car window, hot on the tail of the elusive squirrel. She jerked the car into park, turned off the ignition, and flew out the door. "Rex!" she called to the dog, who was racing after the squirrel down the boardwalk, headed directly toward the main road at the outlet of the marina. Directly toward Tyler's boat.

Tyler saw the fleeing canine zoom by, bounded effortlessly off his boat onto the dock like a gymnast on a pommel horse, glided onto the boardwalk, and followed Rex. When the squirrel dashed up a tree near the end of the boardwalk, leaving Rex pawing at the trunk, Tyler grabbed the dog's collar and knelt, cradling the dog to calm him.

Liz ran to Tyler and Rex, leaping with agility over a knee-high boulder.

"Nice move," Tyler commented as Liz neared. "Like you're a ballerina or something."

"Or something." Liz caught her breath. "Thanks for snagging Rex. I was petrified he'd run into the road. He never watches out for cars."

Tyler stroked Rex's head as the dog settled down. "Cool dog. I like his markings. White and black, like good and bad. With just a little more black than white." He winked at Liz, released his grip on Rex, and stood. "First you let a couple of quarters get away, and now your dog escapes. You need to keep a tighter grip on things," he joked.

"I suppose I do." Liz thought of the grip she was losing on her self-control.

Tyler placed his hands on his hips and looked at her intently. "Take off your sunglasses."

"Beg your pardon?"

"Take off your sunglasses," he repeated, crossing his arms in front of his chest and planting his legs firmly apart.

Liz frowned but complied. She looked at him, feeling the flush rise in her cheeks as she struggled with where to focus her naked eyes.

A broad smile covered his face as he studied her. "Elizabeth Pruitt. When I saw you at the festival, I knew I recognized you from somewhere. I've been racking my brain ever since. Remember me from high school?"

She was almost speechless. Had he really been thinking about her since the festival? He didn't seriously think she'd forgotten the legend, did he? She could just as easily forget Christopher Columbus, Joan of Arc, or Gandhi. "I do remember you, Tyler. Been a long time. I . . . I'm surprised you recognized me." She gazed at him directly, surprising herself for not even thinking to look away.

"Hard to forget someone who sat behind me in homeroom for four years. Let me see, you must have lent me about sixty pens and more pieces of paper than I can count. No matter how many times I asked, you handed them over with a smile. No snarky comments like the other girls made. No obnoxious flirting. And you always wore some really great perfume that smelled like grass and herbs and the outdoors."

He'd actually noticed her back then. Much more than she'd ever thought. Liz had felt invisible for four years, thinking that no one, especially not the hottest boy in school, knew she existed. Yet he had. Nearly fifteen years after that fateful seating arrangement in homeroom, everything was suddenly tumbling into perspective.

"Thank you for catching Rex." Liz was unsure of where to take the conversation. "I'd better get him back to the car before he gets any more urges to run."

"Nothing wrong with a little wanderlust, is there?" The tiny lines that formed in the corners of his eyes just served to make his dimples look more perfect, accenting the spray of freckles that dotted the bridge of his nose and his suntanned cheeks.

"Not that I can see." She returned his smile. From the corner of her eye, Liz saw the squirrel scamper down the tree and make a beeline back toward her car. Before she could move quickly enough to grab Rex, he was racing after the rodent.

"At least he's running in the right direction," called Liz as she hurried after the dog. "Bye, Tyler." She waved as she fled, again jumping over the boulder. She turned around quickly to see him, arms still crossed over his broad chest, nodding approvingly.

The squirrel took refuge under the car, and Rex circled the vehicle, sniffing madly. Liz hoisted him into the car by his collar and rolled up the windows to prevent another escape. She plopped into the driver's seat and let out a *whoosh* as she exhaled.

"Tyler was always a troublesome boy," Grace said calmly, looking straight ahead.

"He's not a boy any longer." Liz started the car and drove down the road, passing Tyler, who stood watching, an impish smile on his face.

He waved as she passed, and she returned the gesture with a shy wiggle of her fingers.

"That doesn't mean he's not still trouble," said Grace.

By the time Liz pulled back into the driveway after their ride to the harbor, she had a dull headache and wanted nothing more than to fix herself an iced tea and sit on the front porch.

Grace had been coolly quiet since their Tyler sighting, and Rex had continued to pace the backseat like a shooting-gallery target, no doubt looking for another squirrel. This was, she feared, an ominous foreboding of the next several months while she lived at her mother's home and ran the dance studio. If a short drive to the harbor produced a headache, she didn't dare imagine how she'd feel by the time her mother had recuperated and Liz was free to move back to Syracuse. There wouldn't be enough aspirin in the free world to dull the pain.

Grace sighed weakly when Liz stopped the car. Liz shot her a glance but offered no reaction; she was in no mood to coddle. She removed Rex from the car and locked him in the backyard before helping Grace inside and settling her in the recliner by the window that overlooked the rose trellis. She gave her a glass of ice water and her poetry books. Grace said softly that she hoped she wasn't too frail to read. Liz forced an impatient grin and walked away, containing the words battling to escape her lips.

Liz, iced tea in hand, trotted to the solitude of the front porch, grabbing the mail from the box before she perched on the top step. No whining mothers, no barking dogs. Just the rerun of her encounter with Tyler playing over and over in her mind.

She kicked off her sandals and let her feet absorb the heat of the wooden steps, as she remembered her mother doing to soothe the ache from dancing. From the top step she glanced over the landscape that had been her world since she was five. How big she used to feel sitting on this top step, perusing her tiny kingdom with a sense of authority. From this vantage point, the whole world was hers for the asking. Maybe someday she'd actually muster the nerve to ask.

On these steps, she'd played with the neighborhood kids, lined up her dolls, and eaten ice cream with her friends and, once in a while, with the thin and perpetually dieting Grace. When Liz was ten, she had fallen down these steps and sprained her wrist. In high school, she and Julie had sat here and talked for hours, sharing their dreams, fears, and fantasies. So many memories for such a small expanse of wood.

Liz rifled through the mail, sorting the stack into toss and keep piles. When she'd reached the end of the stack, she looked at the two piles. The toss pile held a couple of thin fliers from grocery stores and a few catalogs. The keep pile was tottering over with those eerily recognizable business envelopes with cellophane windows. Bills. Way too many bills. By the time she'd opened the last envelope, her hand was shaking and she'd lost track of the amount owed. Too much to add without a calculator.

How would these bills get paid? Even with the income from the summer dance classes Liz was teaching, money would be tight. She placed her head in her hands and curled into a ball, praying for an armored truck to break down in front of the house or an oil geyser to explode through the front lawn.

"What's going on?" asked Julie, causing Liz's head to bolt upright.

"Just having a mental meltdown." She rubbed her temples and tried to remember if the amount of the last bill was $208 or $280. Eight dollars. Eighty dollars. Eight hundred dollars. At this point, what did it matter?

Julie sat on the step next to Liz. "I grabbed your newspaper from the sidewalk."

Liz took the paper, set it beside herself, and made a

mental note to stop the subscription. She had a feeling they'd need that fifty cents a day.

Julie picked up the paper and opened it. "I need to find a new hairdresser," she said, flipping through the pages. "Does my hair look dry to you? When I take off my chef's hat, my hair is so flat."

"The paper always has lots of ads," Liz answered absentmindedly. "You should be able to find someone." She chewed her lip as she stared at the street, seeing nothing.

"Hmm," Julie commented, her petite stature almost hidden behind the full spread of the paper.

"Find one?"

"Not a hairdresser but something you might like." She held the paper in front of Liz's face and pointed to an advertisement. "Here."

"Upstate New York Dance Extravaganza," Liz read aloud. Her eyes quickly skimmed to bold letters in the center of the ad. "Ten thousand dollar grand prize." She sat taller and snatched the paper from Julie, furrowing her brow as she read. "Be part of the first annual contest to uncover the best ballroom dance couple in Upstate New York. On September second, judges will be in Olson to choose the winner of the contest and the ten thousand dollar grand prize. Dance teachers, dance students, and talented amateurs are welcome. To register, call 1-800-DANCE-IT."

"Wow, ten thousand dollars," said Julie. She stretched out her legs and shook them. "Wish I could dance."

Lost in her thoughts, Liz didn't respond. She and the studio could certainly use the money. *If* she had a partner and, *if* she won, she'd have to split the money with him. Two very big *ifs*. But still, five thousand dollars would be enough to get her mother out of the hole—at least start to see daylight—and let Liz return to Syracuse with a clear conscience.

"I wish you could dance too," said Liz. "Then you could disguise yourself as a guy and be my partner." She buried her head back in the paper and reread the ad. Ten thousand dollars was a huge amount of money.

"Why wouldn't you be the guy?" Julie asked. "Is it because my hair is so much shorter than yours?"

"Fine. I'd be the guy." Liz's attention was still on the ad.

"You know ballroom, don't you?"

Liz continued to peruse the ad, barely paying attention to her friend. "I studied it a lot in college, and Mom teaches some classes. It's actually a lot of fun."

"Describe it to me."

Liz surfaced from the black-and-white portal she'd entered. "It's really elegant couples' dancing. Very synchronized and precise. Really brings out the best in the couple. The man and woman have to be in perfect harmony, in sync both physically and emotionally. One of the best ballroom dances is the basic fox-trot. Simple steps done elegantly."

"Simple?" asked Julie. "I never thought dance was simple."

"The steps are really just one, two, three . . . together." Liz moved her hands to imitate feet.

"So find a partner, and enter the contest." Julie opened her arms and shrugged.

"Where am I going to find a guy in Olson who either knows ballroom or can be taught easily? The contest is only five weeks away." Tyler flashed into her mind, and she quickly pushed out the thought. That jumping she'd seen at the festival didn't qualify as ballroom—even if his moves were fluid, graceful, strong, and full of the energy that ballroom required. Even if his posture was straight and his proportions were nearly perfect. Then there was that leap from his boat onto the dock . . .

"Hold an audition," said Julie. "Put an ad in the paper, and hang up fliers."

Liz shook her head. She didn't have high hopes for the offerings that Olson would provide. She bounced her fist off her temple. Here she was, sounding overly critical. Too much like her mother.

"What do you have to lose?" continued Julie. "You may be surprised at what you'll find around here."

Liz thought for a second and then glanced at the stack of bills. "I think I already am."

Chapter Four

"**I**s your mother going to help judge the auditions?"
Julie opened the windows in the Tiptoe Dance Studio,
glanced at herself in the mirror-covered wall, and then
sucked in her stomach, stretching her five-foot-three
height to the max.

"Are you kidding me?" Liz sat on the floor and fastened the buckles on her silver ballroom shoes. She
stood and stepped a few times, acclimating her posture
to the heels, a big change from the flats she usually
wore. Liz raised her arms overhead, bent at the waist,
and stretched forward. Then she bent to the floor and
grabbed her ankles. "I wasn't even going to tell Mom
about the auditions, but I figured she'd get her radar up
if she saw guys coming into the studio. That is, if we

get any takers." She spun around a few times, dissecting her movements in the mirror.

"Doesn't she want you to enter the contest?" Julie straightened the papers on the desk where she planned to sit and sign in the men as they arrived for the auditions.

Liz leaped across the floor, arms extended to the sides, palms upward as if she were holding the most delicate rose in her fingers. She landed on limber feet at the other end of the studio before releasing her pose. "She knows her crummy bookkeeping is the reason I have to enter this contest in the first place. Yet our lovely ballerina puts up a fuss if she thinks the art of dance is being exploited for money." Liz inhaled deeply. "Can't have it both ways, Gracie." She stood tall and bent slightly left, positioning her right hand on the inside of her right knee and forcing her leg to lift to almost vertical. She winced.

"Wish I could do that." Julie raised her short leg just a foot off the floor and almost toppled over. "Good thing chefs only need to be balanced enough to carry platters of food."

"I'm rusty." Liz lowered her leg and let her body fall limp, shaking out the muscles. "Been awhile since I did this type of dancing. I'll have to psych myself up mentally and physically to train for this contest."

"If anyone can do it, you can." Julie moved to the desk and took a seat. "Once a dancer, always a dancer."

"We'll see about that." Liz winked at her friend.

"What about someone who was once a dancer turned dog groomer turned, I guess, dancer again?"

"Still a dancer," Julie added.

"I've been dancing since I could walk, but I'm not a professional. Like Mother," she added, stretching the last word through smacked lips.

"As far as I'm concerned, someone with a fine arts degree in dance and all your training is a professional." Julie poked a pencil into the electric sharpener on the desk, filling the studio with the grind of the sharpener and the distinctive smell of wood and graphite.

"No. Someone with a degree in dance who doesn't get paid to dance is a dog groomer." She pointed to herself and curled her lip.

"So you're a dancing dog groomer turned dance contest participant. What do you have to lose?" Julie stuck another pencil into the sharpener.

Liz held out her arms and threw back her head. "Just all of this," she said, gesturing to the studio. She walked to the ballet barre and lifted her right leg onto it with an easy *swish,* bent her body onto her leg, and stretched.

"Sorry you didn't become a professional dancer?" asked Julie after a slight hesitation. "You know, like a Rockette or someone on Broadway?"

Liz switched to stretch her left leg. "No. I mean, I really liked studying dance at the University of Buffalo, and I always thought I'd become a dance teacher someday."

"So did your mother." Julie ground her third pencil, zipping it into and out of the sharpener several times.

"Plan to do a lot of writing?" Liz lowered her leg, then faced the barre, holding on while she did slow, deep knee bends. She wrinkled her nose at her reflection in the mirror. "Imagine working side by side with my mother. How lovely!" she said sarcastically. "As soon as I turned thirteen and Mom realized my big body would never be right for the ballet stage, she backed off a little. She was all set for me to pick up where she'd left off, or, as she was always fond of telling me, 'For you to resume the career in ballet that motherhood so cruelly robbed me of.'"

Julie opened the desk drawer, smiled when she found a granola bar, and tore off the wrapper, taking a huge bite. "I'm sure she didn't mean it in a crabby way." She wrinkled her nose. "I should have brought over those brownies I baked last night. This is stale."

Liz turned her right side to the barre and slowly lifted her left leg to the side, toe extending to a sharp point. "Yes, she did. Mom did all she could to push me, the square peg, into the round hole of ballet dancing. I took to jazz, tap, and ballroom like a fish to water. Okay, so I was even kind of good at ballet 'for a big-boned girl,' as I was told *ad nauseum*. When she realized I'd never be able to shave my frame to match her statuesque, runway-model-like proportions, she dropped the ballet thing but still thought I'd run this studio with her and teach the other dances."

"Then why'd you go into dog grooming?" Julie wet a fingertip with her tongue and picked up the crumbs that had fallen onto the desk.

"Because dogs don't bite as much as my mother does!" Liz said, unable to suppress a laugh. She moved to the center of the floor, faced the mirror, and ran through a series of time steps with sharp taps of her feet. "There, that feels better. Turn on the stereo, will you?"

The sounds of Cole Porter's "It's De-Lovely" trickled through the room. The soft, steady rhythm kicked off the steps in Liz's head, and the music seeped into her. She listened to each beat, feeling the notes, visualizing the steps until the music floated through her, down to her toes, giving her feet a life of their own.

She poised her arms upward, embracing an invisible partner. Her head tilted slightly over her left shoulder, and she glided about the room. Each step coincided perfectly with a note in the song. She smiled, experiencing the music, living the dance. The studio became a universe where only she existed with her music and her dance.

When the song ended, she dipped slightly backward as if her phantom partner had rested her on a pillow of air. Julie clapped. Liz straightened and faced the mirror, and her head jerked to attention when she caught the reflection of her mother standing in the doorway behind her.

"Shoulders back and arms positioned outward from your chest," said Grace, demonstrating the move as she balanced on her crutches. "High, circular, relaxed arms."

Liz nodded in agreement, stiffening. If she spoke, shooed her mother away, her words would almost certainly incite a war. Leave it to Grace to show up just in time to offer criticism, catch Liz at her less-than-perfect self. Yet it wasn't Grace's unsolicited critique that annoyed Liz; it was the fact that Grace was right. Liz needed to keep her arms poised correctly. That had always been a challenge. When it came to dancing, Grace was always right. In other matters, well, that was another story. But with dance, Grace was the undisputed authority—and she expected to be regarded as just that.

Grace turned to leave through the door connecting the studio to the house, the thump of her crutches echoing in the emptiness of the studio.

"The CD again," Liz said to Julie, motioning to the stereo.

When the music sounded, Liz straightened her shoulders and arched her arms from her chest, holding a soft and high position, and repeated the dance she had just done. Stopping before the song ended, she signaled for Julie to turn off the CD. "I hate it when my mother is right," she snarled.

Julie giggled. "Get used to it. Mothers are always right."

Liz stomped her feet with exaggeration and let out a good-natured laugh. "When do *I* get to be right?"

"You don't. Enough whining. Just keep your eye on the prize, and start dancing," Julie commanded.

Liz crossed her arms and tilted her head toward her friend. "Do I have to tell you who you sound like?"

"So Grace is rubbing off on me." She smirked. "If you think your mother is a problem, just try getting on the bad side of your best friend. Now, pull yourself together. We have a dance contest to win!"

Liz inhaled and glanced at the clock on the wall. Noon. The moment of truth. Time to start the auditions—if anyone showed up. She walked to the front door of the studio, her silver shoes glittering in the sunshine streaming through the open windows. She gasped when she opened the door. A small gathering of men milled outside. "Uh, Julie," she said softly, her gaze still locked on the dozen or so hopeful dancers.

Julie hurried to the door and peered around Liz. "All right! Looks like we have some dancing to do!" She pushed Liz aside, clapped her hands to get the men's attention, and addressed the small crowd. "Welcome, gentlemen. Will the first dancer please step inside and sign in at the desk?"

Liz returned to the center of the dance floor and watched a tall, well-built man who appeared to be about forty approach the desk. He smiled and exchanged pleasantries with Julie. *Not bad,* thought Liz, her hope rising a bit. His physique looked as if it would work well with her stature. He walked well, didn't drag his feet. She pictured him in a tuxedo, à la James Bond. The streaks of gray in his hair would complement the formal look. Okay, she might be able to work with this guy.

Julie motioned for the man to approach Liz in the center of the floor. As he walked toward Liz, he held out his right hand and smiled widely. "George Simon," he said.

Liz returned his firm handshake. "Hi, George. I'm Liz. Thanks for coming. So, you're a dancer?"

"No, I'm a tennis player. Club pro, actually. But I figure anyone can dance. I mean, it can't be that hard, right?" He gestured with open palms.

Liz glanced toward Julie, who was scrunching her nose in response to George's comment. "Music please," she said as her hope drained away.

When "It's De-Lovely" again filled the room, George placed both hands on Liz's shoulders. She repositioned his hands so that his right arm rested on her lower back and his left hand held her right hand. She started moving to the music, but George stayed in place. Liz grinned, and when the right beat sounded, she started to move, this time dragging—literally dragging—George along with a force that could have budged Mount Rushmore. When he finally took a step, he crunched her foot. Then she felt his whole body lock up as if he'd become the Tin Man. Would this song never end? If George played tennis the way he danced, she was going to bet on the opponent.

When the song finally ended and George left, Liz rolled her eyes at Julie, who held up her sign-in sheet and pointed to the big checkmark in the *no* column after George's name.

Liz bent to rub her foot where George had stepped on it. When she straightened up, the next dancer, a man who appeared to be about eighty, was standing next to her. She towered over him by about ten inches. She glanced over to Julie, who shrugged and tried unsuccessfully to keep a smile from breaking out.

"Hello there, darlin'," the elderly man said. He wore plaid Bermuda shorts, a tank top, and a gold chain around his neck. Brown socks sprouted from a pair of wing-tipped shoes and covered his legs up to knobby knees. A few strands of hair made a sweep from above one ear over the bald crown of his head and down to the other ear.

"Hello, sir. My name is Liz. Thank you for coming in." Liz tried to sound pleased.

"My pleasure, darlin'. I'm Benny Burns. My friends call me Featherfoot. Oh, I was the toast of the dance floor years ago when I used to vacation at Grossinger's and The Concord in the Catskills." He placed his hands on his waist and did a few steps. He winked and flashed Liz a smile accented with gold-crowned teeth. "All the ladies wanted a dance with Featherfoot." He reached up and tweaked her nose.

She glanced past Benny's comb-over to see Julie doubled over with laughter, barely able to sit in her chair. Benny wasn't exactly what Liz had been expecting when she'd advertised for a dance partner, but she had to give the guy credit for trying. He may have been the toast of the town years ago, but today he was a few crumbs stuck to the bottom of the toaster.

"Music please," Liz said to Julie, who was wiping tears of laughter from her eyes.

Once again, "It's De-Lovely" wafted throughout the room. Benny put Liz into a clinch, wrapping his arms tightly around her back, resting his head just below her throat. The smell of his hair tonic stung her nose, and he hummed—loudly.

Unlike George, Benny moved Liz around the dance floor, attached to her but not at all to the rhythm of the music.

"Beautiful, right, darlin'?" asked Benny, his eyes closed, his head still plastered to Liz's chest, his behind extended.

"A dance like I've never experienced." Liz chose each word carefully. She waggled her eyebrows in an attempt to motion to Julie to turn off the music, but Julie's head was on the desk to muffle her laughter. Liz tried to move Benny toward the stereo so she could push the off button, but she couldn't budge him from his back-and-forth sway. *Will this song never end?*

When the music finally stopped and Liz was able to pry Benny away from her, she inhaled deeply. "Well, uh, thank you."

"I'll be waitin' for your call, darlin'." Benny winked as he tottered out the door.

"Yes or no?" Julie held up the checklist, a smile bursting onto her face.

"Is there a column that says 'not in a million years'?"

"I guess that's a no." Julie made a dramatic check in the square next to Benny's name, the second of many for the day.

When the last dancer—a burly truck driver passing through town who had apparently listened to too many Broadway musical CDs during his long rides and fancied himself to be a cross between Gene Kelly and Michael Flatley—left the studio, Liz dropped onto her back in the middle of the floor. "Ugh! Rip down the studio sign, and bolt the door shut! Four hours! *Four hours* I've been dancing. My feet were trampled, watch bands were caught in my hair, that high school kid popped his bubble gum on my earring. Uggh!"

Julie sat cross-legged on the floor next to Liz. "Who would have thought there were so many rotten dancers in Olson?"

Liz lifted her head. "I think some of them were looking for a date. How about the John Travolta wannabe with the white suit? That guy was downright creepy." She lowered her head with a thud.

"My favorite was the farmer who showed up in his overalls and muddy boots, reeking of cow." Julie shuddered and pinched her nose with her fingers.

"Don't remind me." Liz sniffed her arm. "I can still smell the cow."

"Now what? You can't dance without a partner."

"I guess I start applying for a job at the grocery store. I have to do something to keep this place afloat." Liz raised her arms. "Isn't there one good male dancer in this whole town? Just one?" she lamented.

Julie grabbed her arm. "Well, there is . . . one."

Chapter Five

"Who?" Liz raised her head from the studio floor just in time to hear a knock on the door. "Who do you know? And who's at the door?"

Julie jumped up and trotted toward the door.

"Unless it's the ghost of Bill 'Bojangles' Robinson, tell whoever it is that auditions are over."

She turned toward the open door and listened. "Saw a light on in here, so I thought I'd drop off your mail instead of putting it into the box," said a voice Liz recognized as Bobby the mailman's. "Wasn't sure it would all fit in the mailbox."

Julie thanked him and shut the door. "Just the mail." She delivered a pile of envelopes to Liz. "That mailman is cute. Can he dance?"

"Bobby?" asked Liz.

"Bobby?" Julie asked in reply. "Now you're on a first-name basis with the cute mailman?" She waggled her eyebrows playfully. "He's a little thin, but I could fatten up those bones with some good cooking. He's built like a dancer."

Liz sighed. "Wish he could dance, but he didn't come for the audition. My guess is, he's more comfortable wearing a mailbag than dance shoes."

"Too bad." Julie rubbed her hands together. "I think he'd look mighty fine in a nice tux and shiny shoes. Almost a tall, thin, Fred Astaire kind of look."

Liz pursed her lips. "I wouldn't wish this dance stuff on a nice guy like Bobby. He's better off sticking to his mail route. Much better off."

She rolled to a sitting position and sifted through the pile. She pursed her lips and plopped back to a sprawl, letting the mail fall from her hands and scatter on the floor. "Bills, bills, and more bills." She threw a hand over her eyes, reminding herself of her mother's dramatic stage moves.

Julie picked up a flyer. "Here's an announcement about the new otter exhibit at the zoo. Not everything's a bill."

Liz unmasked her eyes and squinted at her friend. "Okay, so there's one announcement from the zoo and twenty thousand bills."

"Just trying to be optimistic." Julie grinned. "It's not totally hopeless."

"Maybe I can get a job at the zoo," Liz whined.

"You won't have to if you find the right dance partner." Julie straightened the mail back into a tall pile that quickly toppled over.

"And we all know how well that's working out," Liz said sarcastically.

"As I said, there is one other dancer."

"No," Liz said quickly. She knew who Julie was thinking about. He was the first thought that had run through her mind when she'd decided to enter the contest. His was the one face she had hoped to see in the line-up outside the studio for an audition. He was all she could think of as she went through the paces with the stick-thin, middle-aged man who hopped like a kangaroo and sang loudly during the audition.

"No, what?" asked Julie.

Liz cleared her throat. "Just no."

"No?"

"No, I am *not* going to ask Tyler Augustine to dance with me." Liz clapped her hands in one emphatic beat.

"Why not? You know he's the best dancer in town. Plus he's gorgeous and energetic and would win the hearts of the judges."

Liz pondered her friend's words. Julie was right on all counts. The thought had floated through her own head a million times. When she had seen the ad for the contest, she'd known then that the only chance she had to win was to make Tyler part of her program. He was the only solution. He was also the only problem. How could she ever ask him to be her partner?

"You know I can't ask Tyler to dance with me."

"Why not?" Julie shrugged. "You walk up to him and say 'Want to dance with me?' What's so hard about that? Why can't you say that?"

"Well, you know, uh, he's . . . I just can't. Forget it."

Julie gathered up the stack of bills and held them in one hand. She held out her other hand, mimicking a scale. "Tyler," she said, lifting the empty hand. "Job at the grocery store or zoo," she continued, lifting the hand full of envelopes. "The best choice isn't always the easiest choice."

Liz scrunched her eyes closed and rubbed her temples. "I hate it when you make sense." She sighed. "Okay, okay. I'll ask him."

"Best idea I've heard all day." Julie clapped.

"Or maybe the riskiest," Liz said.

"Looks like you just took a long overdue step closer to the danger zone," said Julie with a wink.

After dinner that evening, Liz put Rex into the car and drove to the harbor. Since Julie had convinced her to go ahead with this absurd idea, she'd been going over and over her plan to ask Tyler. She needed to act nonchalant, confident, and assertive, none of which were in her repertoire of personal characteristics. She decided to park on the far end of the harbor, away from Tyler's boat, leash up Rex, and then walk casually down the boardwalk by his boat. After all, everyone strolled around the harbor. Tyler would never suspect she was looking for him. He'd just think she was walking her dog on a lovely summer evening, right? If he wasn't on his boat, that would be a sign for Liz to start learning how to pack bags at the grocery store or clean out cages at the zoo. And if he was there . . .

With her plan firm, she let Rex lead the way down the boardwalk. Liz exchanged nods with passersby, looking as if she was merely a passerby herself. All systems were go, and her confidence grew. Liz picked up her pace and neared Tyler's boat, convinced she didn't look like she was about to grovel for his help. Maybe Julie had been right about her being overdue to approach the danger zone, which didn't look at all dangerous from this vantage point. So far, so good.

Until a chipmunk scurried from the base of a fallen tree and scooted with lightning speed in front of her and Rex. The dog started barking madly and yanked so hard on his leash that Liz, hanging on with two hands, was barely able to contain him. "Shh!" she hissed. Of all places for Rex to lose it. "Rexie, quiet," she croaked, trying to keep her voice as muffled as possible.

The more she tried to quiet Rex, the louder he barked, even though the chipmunk had long since disappeared. She averted her eyes from Tyler's boat, fearing the barking dog would blow her cover and expose her true intentions.

Rex pulled Liz past Tyler's boat. She glanced out the corner of her eye. No sign of him. She sighed with relief. At least he hadn't witnessed the cartoonish scene of Rex dragging her, trying with all his might to shake free of the iron grip she had on the leather leash.

Then disappointment washed away the embarrassment. Tyler wasn't there. As nervous as she was to see him, to appear too eager to ask him to dance with her, she was more upset to realize she'd missed her chance. Not just a chance to dance but a chance. Maybe she could learn to like arranging tomatoes into a tall, balanced pyramid or come to appreciate the earthy fragrance of baboons. Her stomach lurched when she remembered the dancing cattle farmer.

Just as she had brought Rex to a halt, she heard her name and turned to see Tyler ascend the stairs from the galley of the boat and step onto the deck.

"Thought I recognized that bark." He planted his feet on deck. He was wearing a dirty T-shirt and rumpled cargo shorts. His black, oil-stained hands held some mechanical, metal part. He winked and flashed her a smile complete with a dirt-smudged dimple. "And now I recognize the lady."

"Sorry if Rex bothered you." Liz bent to pet the dog, who had finally calmed down.

Tyler arched his eyebrows and shot her a crooked smile. "Another squirrel?"

"Chipmunk this time."

Tyler laughed. "At least he doesn't discriminate among rodents."

Rex let out a yip as if he knew he was the topic of conversation.

Tyler lifted the greasy part in his hand. "Say, I was just about to quit working on this carburetor and have a soda. Come on board and join me." His invitation was infused with the air of a gentle command.

"Well, uh, yeah, sure," Liz stuttered, caught off guard by the turn of events.

"Tie Rex to that railing, where we can keep an eye on him, before he bolts off after any more wildlife." Tyler pointed to a waist-high wooden railing paralleling the boardwalk.

When the dog was secured, Liz neared the boat. Tyler set down the engine part, picked up a rag that looked as greasy as his shirt, wiped his hands, and then reached for her.

"I saw you take a flying leap over that rock the other day, so I know those long legs can reach the deck." He grabbed her hand, hoisting her up with an easy tug.

Once on deck, Liz steadied her foothold, feeling the gentle rocking of the boat beneath her. She surveyed the immaculate surroundings, the bright white deck shimmering even as dusk attempted to settle over the sky. Beyond the boat, the blue-black harbor gave way to glorious Lake Ontario, an ominous, massive body of water singing its siren's song to anyone awed by nature and never failing to enchant with its peace and power.

"Spend much time on the water?" Tyler pulled the greasy T-shirt over his head like a snake shedding its skin, rumpled it into a ball, and tossed it down into the galley. He grabbed a clean, blue tee from the seat and slipped into it, letting it fall over his tanned, muscular chest. "That's better."

"Uh-huh." Liz inhaled deeply. She wasn't sure what was better, but something certainly was.

When the boat in the next slip pulled out, it created a gentle wake, surprising Liz and causing her to stumble toward Tyler. He reached out with both arms and caught her, steadying her as they stood nose to nose.

"Good thing I was standing here, or you'd be taking a dip," said Tyler with Liz still just inches from his face. "I should have warned you to watch your balance."

She smiled shyly and resumed her stance, even though she was in no hurry to have Tyler loosen his firm grip. "So first you catch my dog, and then you catch me. I guess I owe you two debts of gratitude."

He nodded and smiled widely. "I'll keep that in mind." He took her elbow and guided her to a seat. "You'd better stay put while I get us a couple of sodas. I don't want to take the chance you'll trip and break one of those long legs. Now *that* would be a shame." He winked and disappeared into the galley, leaving Liz motionless until he resurfaced a minute later with two cans of soda.

Liz thought of her mother's broken leg, took a can, and downed a big, fuzzy mouthful of non-diet soda, a rare treat. Tyler apparently didn't have to worry that sugar intake would ruin his well-toned physique.

"So we meet again, Elizabeth Pruitt." Tyler leaned on the side of the boat across from Liz's seat. "Haven't seen you in a dozen years, and now I see you every place I go. Not that I'm complaining." He ran a hand through his thick blond hair.

"Funny how that happens," she replied, carefully choosing her words.

"So what brings you back to the harbor?" Tyler appeared to drain half his can with a quick swig.

Liz shuffled her feet. "Well, uh . . . I . . . I thought I might like to book a fishing charter. You know, fish for, uh, for flounder."

Tyler roared. "Flounder? In Lake Ontario? I always knew you were a smartie, Liz, but I didn't think you were a comedian too. That's a good one—flounder."

"Well, what kind of fish could you help me catch?" Liz's total ignorance of fishing was coming through loud and clear, and she'd only uttered one sentence. She wasn't used to sounding so clueless, and she scolded herself for not coming up with a better story. One that didn't accentuate her ignorance about fishing.

"Right now, nothing. My boat isn't working; so until I get this engine running, the only fish I can offer you is a can of tuna."

"Oh, I see."

"Yeah, kind of a catch-22. I can't get the motor fixed until I make some money with a charter, and I can't run a charter until the motor is fixed." Tyler raised his can. "So I sit here and drink soda instead." He winked. "At least I'm in good company."

Liz nodded, happy to accept what she thought was a compliment but finding it difficult to concentrate on the conversation as her mind grappled with how to bring up the subject of the dance contest. She'd hoped to get him talking about his line of work and then interject her story about her mother's dance studio. So much for that disastrous idea. "So, what have you been doing since high school?" she asked, for lack of anything else to say.

Tyler took another long drag on his soda, draining the can. "This and that, here and there." He grinned widely. "You know, just stuff."

"Sounds fascinating." Liz purposely injected sarcasm into her tone even though, in reality, Tyler's *stuff* had almost certainly been more fascinating than her dog-grooming business.

He shrugged. "All depends on what angle you look at it from. Suppose it's been more exciting than if I'd stayed in Olson. Then again, who knows?"

"Why did you leave town after graduation?" She hoped she wasn't getting too personal, but Tyler seemed so easy to talk to, as if they've known each other for years. They did, Liz reminded herself. Just that there was a difference between knowing and *knowing*.

He laughed. "That need to experience life in the fast lane. Get some excitement into my life. Always on the lookout for something better than I could find in my own backyard. You leave too?"

"For college." Liz wasn't about to add that she had needed a break from her mother.

"Figured a brain like you went to college," he said.

"You and school seemed to be a good pair." He tucked his shirt into his shorts.

Liz guessed this was a compliment, yet she didn't feel flattered, remembering all those dateless Saturday nights she'd spent with her textbooks. "What brings you back to Olson?" She turned the conversation back to Tyler.

"Family. I came back a few months ago, right before my grandfather died. I've been meaning to leave again; but now that my boat's on the fritz, I'm kind of stuck here."

"Sorry to hear about your grandfather." So the story Grace had heard was accurate. Well, she had to give the guy credit for being a concerned grandson. But what was the story with the lack of money to fix his boat? The Augustine family was a pillar of the community and had a history of old money and blue blood. Judging from the homestead, the nice cars, and the prosperous family banking business, money had never been a problem for the Augustines.

"Thanks. How about you? Move back after college?" He hiked himself onto the side of the boat.

"Actually, I'm just back temporarily. I live in Syracuse, but my mother broke her leg, so I'm helping out for a while." She felt the conversation inching to where she wanted it to go.

"Helping out your mom," he said with a slow nod. "Always knew you were a nice girl, Liz. That put you way out of my league in high school."

Out of *his* league? Liz didn't think she was *in* any league, let alone *out* of his. Tyler was the untouchable legend, not her. Her eyebrows slipped into a *V*.

He laughed at her reaction. "Come on. Don't tell me you didn't know that ninety percent of the guys in our school had the hots for you but were afraid to ask you out because you were so much better than they were. You were one of those perfect girls all the guys shied away from." He shrugged. "Thanks to girls like you, the cheerleaders, class-cutters, and curfew-breakers got more dates."

Liz scrunched her nose. "Are you sure you're thinking about the right girl? Was there more than one Liz Pruitt in our class? I was the tall girl with the braces. Library club. Yearbook editor. Homecoming-dance cleanup committee."

He bent toward her, legs dangling, muscular arms gripping the side. "Everyone knew you were a diamond in the rough. Good looks, brains. Sure to turn out the best. You were the most challenging kind."

Challenging? Best? What was he talking about? She didn't remember too many guys who'd acted like she even existed.

"You and your friend—what was her name?—Julie something."

"Julie Baines," Liz interjected.

"Yeah, Julie." Tyler raised his eyes upward. "The guys used to wonder who would end up playing Romeo to the lovely little Julie-ette. But you two were too interested in your clubs, volunteering at church, and doing your homework to notice us."

Liz waved off his comment with a flick of her hand. Was it true that all those dateless Saturdays she and Julie had spent playing Scrabble and baking cookies could have been filled with dances and rides to the ice cream shop if they'd just paid attention? Although Liz was intrigued by Tyler's comment, she didn't think he was very accurate. After all, she'd been the one to live in her skin, not him. Wouldn't she have noticed if a boy had shown any interest? The years since high school hadn't proved too eventful in the romance department either. A few short-lived relationships and the occasional casual date were certainly nothing to crow about.

"Quiet evening," Liz commented, eager to change the subject.

" 'Bout as rowdy as it gets around here," Tyler replied. "Now that Ontario Fest is over, Olson will ride out the rest of the summer and then make a quiet segue into fall before it gets buried alive in winter."

This was her chance. Liz had to ask him. She had to get this over with. "So, you had fun at the festival?" Her mouth felt dry, and she fought the instinct to avert her gaze from Tyler's.

"Oh, yeah." He hopped off the gunwale. "I don't get back too often for the festival, but this year I ran into some old friends and had a chance to shake things up a bit." He did a little jump and a spin, and causing the boat to lurch. "Got in a little dance action, and it felt mighty good."

"I noticed," Liz blurted out.

Tyler opened his eyes widely and snapped his gaze to her. "You saw me dance?"

Liz, silent, bobbed her head.

He arched his eyebrows and grinned, dimples growing bigger by the second. He crouched down, meeting Liz eye to eye. "What did you think?"

She sat straighter, backing away. "You were very . . . uh, very lively." She twisted a lock of hair that had fallen forward over her shoulder.

"You like to dance?"

If she'd danced in the high school plays as her mother had prodded her to do or done more than huddle against the wall during the few dances she'd attended with Julie, perhaps Tyler would know that dancing was her second skin. Then again, she didn't imagine he'd attended too many drama club plays, and he was too cool to spend much time inside the high school gymnasium during school dances. "Yes."

He reached over and flipped on a CD player perched on the fish locker. The Rolling Stones' "(I Can't Get No) Satisfaction" filled the air. Tyler pulled Liz to her feet and began dancing, moving and dipping to the music in a style reminiscent of his carefree, natural moves at the festival. Only this time he was closer. Much closer.

After a few measures, she joined him. Liz felt the

music flow through her like a magic elixir, the way it always did, willing her to dance, giving her freedom to feel the joy. To break free from herself. It unleashed her soul.

They smiled and shook, circling each other and turning purely random movements into something that looked close to being a choreographed dance. Liz interjected steps she'd learned in college, and Tyler responded beautifully. He seemed to sense her next move, anticipate the next step, mirror her movements with his own lead. When Liz moved a shoulder toward him, he backed up and then moved into her. When she moved her feet in a simple four-four rhythm, he responded in kind, complementing the pattern, interjecting his own twists that Liz, in turn, easily mimicked.

He had passed the test.

They turned their backs to each other, maintaining the sprightly rhythm. Liz was joyous at her discovery. Tyler really was a fantastic dancer. He not only looked right on the dance floor, he had a knack, a true knack, for feeling the dance, experiencing the moment. Even her mother would have been impressed. She reveled in her find, gazing at the darkening horizon, acclimating to the sway of the boat. Dancing. Dancing with Tyler Augustine.

When Liz turned back to him, heady with hope and feet in overdrive, Tyler stood facing her, hands on his hips. She stopped.

"Why, Liz Pruitt." He smirked. "You really can

dance. I mean *really*. Pretty awesome. Are you a pro or something?"

"My mother owns the Tiptoe Dance Studio. I've been dancing my whole life." She felt a great need to come clean.

"Now this is starting to make sense." He nodded deeply and slowly as he cogitated. "You're just full of surprises, aren't you?"

She straightened the short sleeves of her pink blouse and inhaled. "Dance with me, Tyler. In a contest. Be my partner." The words raced from her lips. There, she'd said it.

"What?" He wrinkled his forehead. "Dance contest?"

She reached out a hand but didn't touch him. "I need a partner for a dance contest, Tyler. I want you to be my partner." She forced herself to stand strong, not falter or back down.

He rolled back his head and roared. "Hey, just because I can shake a mean leg doesn't mean I'd enter any dance contest. No way. That is not my style." He sliced the air with a swish of his hand.

"But you're good," Liz persisted. "You're great, actually. We could win."

"So what? I dance for fun, not to win a medal." He crossed his arms in front of his chest, looking at Liz straight on as if daring her to challenge him.

"No medal. Five thousand dollars." She was pointed, placing her chips on the table. She was, after all, here to make a business deal with Tyler, not form a relationship or impress him. Wasn't she?

Tyler tilted his head toward her. "Five thousand dollars?"

"Ten thousand dollar grand prize. If we win, we split, fifty-fifty. I'll choreograph the dance, get the costumes, pick the music. It won't cost you a thing."

He was silent, and Liz knew she'd piqued his interest.

"Plus it could be fun," she added, not sure how attractive this last bid was. Her idea of fun might not be anywhere near his.

"Costume? What kind of dance are you talking about?"

"Ballroom. It's the thing these days." She clenched her hands. "Everyone is doing it."

Tyler laughed again and stomped a foot in amusement. "You almost had me, Liz. But ballroom? I've seen that dancing. The guys wear a tuxedo, shiny shoes. They have their snooty noses in the air. Not this guy. Not even for five grand. You're going to have to do better than that."

Unfortunately, she didn't have anything better to offer.

Chapter Six

"Your father expected you for dinner." Agnes glanced over her shoulder at Tyler as he walked through the kitchen door, dropped his duffel bag on the floor, and tossed his keys onto the countertop. She reached down to continue scrubbing the dishes in the suds-filled sink, raising a few bubbles to float around her head.

Tyler placed an arm around her shoulders, and she leaned into him with maternal affection. "How was your day, Agnes?" He plopped into a heavy captain's chair at the kitchen table.

Agnes pulled the plug, and the soapy water slipped down the drain in a sucking spiral. "Good, honey. He waited until seven-thirty and then asked me to serve dinner without you." She hastily wiped her hands, red and moist, on the dish towel slung over her shoulder.

Tyler shrugged and reached for one of the peanut-butter cookies piled high on a plate in the middle of the table. "I was busy."

"You know your father likes a phone call if you won't be home as planned. He's on a schedule." Agnes took a cellophane-covered dinner plate from the refrigerator and popped it into the microwave. "Hungry?" she asked, after the fact.

"Always." Tyler reached for another cookie. "Well, that's the catch, Agnes." He pointed with the cookie and then took a bite. "I'm not really home."

"Your father would beg to differ with you." She placed her hands on her hips and studied the microwave, watching the plate rotate and the seconds count down before turning back to Tyler. "This is where you grew up, and you've been living here for three months. So as far as he's concerned, you're home. You'll spoil your dinner," said Agnes as Tyler took another bite of the cookie.

"This stomach has always had plenty of room for your home cooking." Tyler patted his midsection playfully. "Chances are, a whole roomful of cookies wouldn't spoil my appetite." He inhaled deeply. "Whatever you're warming up is making my mouth water."

The microwave bell rang, and Agnes delivered the steaming plate to Tyler and arranged a place setting on a napkin. "Now, eat before this gets cold." She pinched his cheek before pouring herself a cup of coffee and sitting across from him at the table.

Tyler took a forkful of pork tenderloin, chewed, and licked his lips. "Awesome. If I'd had known that pork this tender was waiting for me, I'd have made sure to be home in time for dinner." He stabbed another forkful, dipped it in gravy, and shoveled it into his mouth. "Talk about hog heaven. Literally."

Agnes took a sip of coffee. "I'm sure your father wants you to be home on time for dinner, pork or not." She reached to the middle of the table and arranged the condiments on the lazy susan.

"A guy who's almost thirty should be able to decide his own schedule," said Tyler, his mouth full, a drop of gravy on his chin. He pushed his chair closer, placed his elbows on top of the table, and ate with gusto.

"That's not what your father would say. You know he likes structure, control."

"Whatever." Tyler attacked a mound of mashed potatoes, causing a small avalanche of butter. "You know him better than I do." He looked over at the counter. "Any more gravy?"

Agnes retrieved a gravy boat from the refrigerator and popped it into the microwave. While she waited for it to heat, she poured Tyler a tall glass of milk, then leaned against the cupboard and crossed her arms, her apron tied high over her plump tummy. "Like I always told you, honey, it's better to keep the peace than make war."

He laughed. "Are you sure the saying isn't 'All's fair in love and war'?" He was surprised when Liz flashed through his mind—a vision of her sitting on the boat, the setting sun catching the glistening auburn highlights in her hair, her long legs crossed casually at the ankles, freckles dusting her nose; her smile a mix of shyness and revelation that she'd found him out.

When the microwave rang, Agnes grabbed the hot gravy boat with the hem of her apron and poured the thick topping onto Tyler's pork. "Enough?"

"Perfect, as always."

She set down the gravy boat in front of him and took her seat again. "What was so important that kept you away from dinner?"

"Kind of a crazy thing." He scooped peas onto his fork, losing a few as they rolled off the tines. "This girl I knew in high school stopped by the marina, and we got to talking." *And dancing.* "Lost track of the time." *Because I found it hard to take my eyes off of her.* "Remember Liz Pruitt?"

"Oh, yes. Grace's daughter. When I was at the beauty shop the other day, I heard that Grace had broken her leg and that her daughter was back in town to help her." Agnes stirred another teaspoon of sugar into her coffee.

"Haven't seen Liz since we graduated, and within the last couple of days I've run into her a few times." Tyler reached for a slice of bread and soaked up the gravy on his plate.

"I last saw Liz about a year ago. She was with her mother at the farmer's market. Such a beautiful girl," Agnes commented. "And so sweet. A sturdier version of her mother. More comfortable and real. Less pomp and circumstance."

Tyler nodded, the loaded fork suspended before his open mouth. *Sturdy.* Now that was a word he wouldn't think of to describe her. If *sturdy* meant tall, strong, and perfectly proportioned, then Agnes was right. Were Liz's eyes smoky brown, or did they have amber flecks around the outer ring? Or maybe she was wearing contact lenses. Didn't she wear glasses throughout high school?

"Something wrong with the pork?"

"No, no," he said quickly, pushing aside his thoughts to resume eating, chewing quickly as if to make up for lost time.

"So, what did Liz have to say?"

Tyler wiped his mouth with the back of one hand. "You won't believe this. She wants me to be in a dance contest with her. How wacky is that?" He took a long drink of milk.

"Why is that so wacky? You're a fantastic dancer. When you were little, we used to spend hours dancing before you went to sleep at night. You'd hike your little feet onto mine, and we'd twirl around your bedroom like there was no tomorrow." Agnes smiled fondly. "Remember how your father wanted you to sit quietly and work on a jigsaw puzzle or read before bed? All you wanted to do was dance. I'd put on my slippers so my clodhopper feet wouldn't sound like a runaway train on the ceiling above your father's den. And we'd dance and dance until I had to bribe you with a snack to go to bed." She giggled. "You were such a little sweetheart."

"Good times, Agnes. Good times." Tyler pushed back his empty plate and brushed a few crumbs from his shirt. He rubbed his stomach with satisfaction. "Thanks for that fantastic meal. You're a wizard in the kitchen."

"So why don't you dance with Liz? Might be fun."

He shook his head and pointed a backward thumb at himself. "This guy doesn't do dance contests."

"Well, that's one statement your father *would* approve of." Agnes scooped crumbs from the table into the palm of her hand and tossed them into the sink.

Tyler snickered. "Yeah, the old man sure would get his feathers ruffled if I entered a dance contest."

"Well, then, you sure wouldn't want to do it and upset him." Agnes raised her eyebrows and batted her eyelashes. She stood, cleared away Tyler's plate, and refilled his glass of milk. "May as well finish those cookies." She bent and gave him a kiss on the head. " 'Night, honey. I'm going to my room to finish knitting my afghan."

Tyler grabbed her hand. "Thanks again for dinner, Agnes. My favorite."

"Me or the pork?" she asked with a wink.

Tyler sat alone in the kitchen, slouched with one leg slung over the arm of the chair. He stuffed in his fourth peanut-butter cookie, taking in the familiar tick of the old rooster clock. He vaguely remembered being about four years old when his mother used to tell him with a wink and that funny way she crinkled up her nose to get to bed on time or else Mr. Rooster would crow. And Mr. Rooster would get angry if he had to crow at night instead of in the morning. His throat tightened at the thought of that fading, precious memory.

He surveyed the room, alive with the memories of Agnes pulling a pan of brownies from the oven, chaotic holiday-dinner preparations, and school friends perched on the counters as they swapped war stories of football practice, embellished tales of their dates, and feasted on any leftovers they could find. This kitchen had been the center of his life for eighteen years—and a place he'd visited infrequently for the past eleven.

Aside from the updated appliances and new granite countertop, nothing much had changed. The lid on the tea canister was glued together, a war wound from the toy car that had fallen from Tyler's pocket as he had balanced on the countertop and reached high into the top cupboard to rummage for candy. The small corner shelf held an array of knickknacks, including the bell-shaped salt and pepper shakers he'd given Agnes one Christmas. Same old, same old. Yet totally different.

"So, you are home." Samuel Augustine entered the kitchen, stealing Tyler back from the past. He pulled a napkin from the holder on the counter, took off his glasses, and wiped the lenses with slow, deliberate circles.

"Yep," Tyler replied. "I'm here." He drummed the table.

"You missed a fine dinner." Sam continued to clean his glasses, not looking at Tyler. "A fine dinner indeed."

"Just finished it. Actually, I didn't miss a thing at all."

Sam looked at his son. "After all these years, don't tell me that Agnes is still caring for you." He forced a little "Humpf."

Tyler puffed out his lips, exasperated. He wasn't about to go there again. Not this time. Not while his mind kept flashing back to his visit with Liz, who, for some reason, wouldn't stop buzzing around his brain.

Sam put on his glasses and leaned against the counter, stuffing his hands into the pockets of his brown cardigan sweater. "Spend the day on your boat . . . or elsewhere?" His tone offered no hint at the reason for his question.

"Mostly on the boat," Tyler replied. "Good weather today." He almost laughed aloud, listening to himself speak to his father in polite, neutral terms as if they were strangers on a bus. As if the conversation was just a collection of empty words, meaningless, meant to fill dead air. Perhaps all those years of being told the virtues of silence had given Tyler the idea that conversation wasn't high on his father's list of preferred activities.

Sam nodded. "Yes, yes, it was lovely. Were you out on a charter today? I noticed the lake was quite calm when I drove to the bank this morning."

Was his father really trying to talk, just talk? If so, Tyler had to temper his own contribution to the dialog, keep the flames burning low. Pleasantly surprised at his father's efforts, he chose his words carefully.

"No charters today. Couldn't."

"Couldn't?" Sam placed a hand under his chin, a finger resting vertically over his mouth as if he were questioning the worth of a piece of art in a gallery.

Tyler exhaled loudly, releasing . . . everything. "Trouble with the boat's motor. Big-time."

Sam nodded, finger still in place. "I see. Are you going to have it repaired? Or is this a sign that—"

"Repaired," Tyler said quickly, the word forming an invisible barrier between his raw emotions and the accusations he anticipated. He put his hands together and clenched them tightly, pushing away the frustration before it engulfed him. He wouldn't let his father get the best of him. Not today, when his mind was occupied with other things, with someone else. "Problem is, the repairs will cost a few thousand dollars. Not in my budget right now."

Sam raised his eyebrows, then sat at the table next to his son. He folded his hands on the tabletop and leaned close to Tyler like a counselor connecting with a client. "Problem is, you don't have a budget, Tyler. I'm a banker. All the Augustines until . . . well, until you, have been bankers. I know about money. I can help you."

Tyler twisted his mouth and ran his fingers through his hair. He leaned back his head before sitting upright.

"Dad, we've been through this before. Your idea of help is for me to get a job at your bank and give up my charter business. No can do."

"Your choice." Sam pursed his lips under his graying mustache. "You're a man, Tyler. I can't decide your fate for you."

"What about a bank loan?"

Sam snickered, raising his eyebrows so that his forehead wrinkled and pushed his receding hairline even farther back. "To be eligible for a loan, you have to have a job, collateral, stability. Without those things, not even the son of the bank president can get a loan."

Tyler rubbed his face. He didn't want to ask, and he already knew the answer, but he'd never been afraid to take a chance. "Then how about a loan from you personally instead of the bank?"

Sam smirked. "Would this loan be similar to the loan for the motorcycle and the backpacking through France and the fishing trip to Argentina and . . ."

Tyler held up a hand to quiet his father. "Okay, okay. I get it." He turned away.

Sam touched his arm. Tyler caught his breath, taken aback by the unexpected contact. Sam was quiet until Tyler turned to him.

"Son, the money isn't the issue. Your wanton lifestyle is. The roaming around the world, lack of a career path, dismissal of responsibility are just not good for anyone. Especially not an Augustine."

Tyler leaned closer to his father. Closer than he'd

been since—he couldn't remember when. "You know I want to be a fisherman, a charter captain. People do make a living at it. A good living. I know I can too. Gramp and I shared a love of the water, of fishing."

Sam smiled. "You certainly were the apple of your grandfather's eye. No doubt about that." He sat straighter and cleared his throat. "I know I haven't said this, but it really meant a lot to him, to me, for you to come back home and spend those last precious months with him. You were a good grandson to do that, Tyler. A good man."

Tyler was speechless. His father never expressed such emotion. Not when Tyler was named Athlete of the Year in high school. Not when he received a full scholarship to college. Definitely not when he forfeited the scholarship to travel. Not when his mother had died when Tyler was four. Why now? Had the loss of his father given Sam reason to reconsider his life, to try to better understand what was important? "Gramp meant a lot to me," Tyler finally said, his voice strained. "A lot."

"Your grandfather loved you, and he would have enjoyed seeing you turn thirty and become eligible for the Augustine Trust. Six months ago, when you turned twenty-nine, he told me he was counting down the days until you reached that milestone. A very important event in the life of an Augustine." Sam raised his eyebrows. "Actually, considering the, um, situation, I'm not sure how he would have reacted to your turning thirty."

"Augustine Trust?" Tyler furrowed his brow. "Situation?"

Sam stood and walked to the refrigerator. He took out a bottle of soda and then reached for two clean glasses from a cupboard. He poured the soda, sat back at the table, and handed a glass to Tyler. "Cheers, son," he said, hoisting his glass for a toast.

"Cheers? Okay, Dad. You've lost me."

"Up with the glass, son." A smile crept over Sam's face. "The only thing more prestigious than being an Augustine is being a thirty-year-old Augustine, as you'll be in just six months."

Tyler clinked his soda glass with his father's, still wondering what was going on and how the conversation had gone from accusation to scolding to toasting. All too weird, even for the Augustine household.

His father set down his glass and refolded his hands on the table, an air of propriety overtaking him as he prepared to speak. "For generations, our family has protected its wealth and ensured its continuation through the Augustine Trust. This very special trust states that at the age of thirty, every Augustine who is a direct descendent of Maximilian Horace Crestfield Augustine, my great-grandfather, is to receive a ten thousand dollar advance on inheritance as a gesture of good faith and family honor—provided that two very important requirements are met."

Tyler latched on to the sound of ten thousand dollars

and twitched in his chair. That was a formidable sum of money for anyone, but to a guy whose wallet held only enough money to fill the gas tank of his motorcycle, it sounded like a treasure trove. That money would more than fix his boat; it would give him a chance to get his charter business up and running. And let him honor his grandfather in the only way he knew how. He sat upright and locked his gaze on his father, eager to hear more. "I'll be thirty in six months."

Sam nodded. "That's just one stipulation."

"And the other?" Tyler was ready to shave his head or donate a body part if necessary. *Just please don't ask me to give up the boat and fishing.* That was his only remaining connection to his grandfather, his idol.

Sam sat back and perched his hands into a steeple in front of his chest, an interviewer assessing whether the applicant was up to par.

Tyler was almost out of his skin as he waited for his father's words. Admittedly, the setup sounded archaic and a bit bizarre. And it went hand in hand with the crazy expression on the face of Great-great-grandfather Max in the painting in his father's library, but he wouldn't question good fortune. After all, he was an Augustine. "What is it?"

"Well," began Sam, choosing his words carefully. "The recipient of the trust must also be married or have, uh, intentions and plans to propagate the next generation."

Tyler fought the impulse to jump up from his chair

and declare that old Max must have been one insane dude. "Married? Next generation?"

"You see, Max was an only child. And the thought of being the end of the line, the end of our great family, was devastating to him. This trust was his way to ensure the Augustines would make their mark for generations and generations." Sam reached for Tyler's arm and patted it before quickly pulling back his hand. "Sorry, son. I know the marriage stipulation makes you ineligible for the trust."

Tyler felt his mind kick into overdrive, and his eyes flicked back and forth. His breathing quickened, and he patted the table with an uneven rhythm and shifted his weight in the chair. "I'm engaged." The words escaped with an unknown force. "My fiancée and I can, uh, move up our plans and get married within six months, by the time I'm thirty, to comply with the trust."

Sam's face blanked, and he cocked his head toward Tyler. "You're engaged?"

Panic rose from Tyler's toes and traveled to his head, and he grasped for the right words—any words, actually—to fabricate his story. "Well, with everything going on with Gramp, I . . . I just didn't think it was right to bring up." He sent his grandfather a little thought of apology, knowing the dear man would actually be proud of his grandson for being so resourceful and gutsy—*and* for pulling a fast one on Sam. Gramp's favorite pastime had been getting Sam into a tizzy.

Sam raised his soda glass in another toast. "Well,

that's wonderful, son! As keeper of the trust, I suppose I could even give you a few more months of wiggle room, if you need a little more time to plan the wedding, make it a grand affair, make sure our family in Europe can attend. I could give you your ten thousand dollars on your thirtieth birthday," said Sam, looking at Tyler over his glasses, "as long as we know wedding plans are well under way."

Tyler should be happy for the concession, but it really didn't solve his immediate problem—the lack of a fiancée.

"So, who is my future daughter-in-law?" Sam smiled widely.

The words slipped out before Tyler had a chance to reconsider, to discard the lie before it became any more monstrous and devoured what was left of his soul. "Liz. Elizabeth Pruitt." He stopped breathing.

"The lovely young woman you knew in high school? Grace's daughter?" Sam looked puzzled but pleased. "I had no idea you'd kept in contact with her."

"She's the one." Tyler gulped.

"The daughter of a prima ballerina, a fine and well-bred young lady . . . yes, Liz will be a marvelous addition to the Augustine family. Good choice, Tyler." Sam held his glass high. "Well, here's to you and Liz. This is quite unexpected but exciting news."

Tyler raised his glass slowly and clinked it on his father's, forcing a smile. "You can say that again!"

Chapter Seven

Tyler walked quietly up to the door of the Tiptoe Dance Studio. Finding it open, he looked inside. There, with her back to him, Liz grasped the barre and stretched one leg upward as a jazzy tune filled the studio. Tyler had only seen dancers raise their legs that high on television, but those gorgeous, leggy women seemed to be more fantasy than reality.

Like Liz.

Women who carried themselves with elegance and strength.

Like Liz.

Women whose dance ability coupled with their beauty to create an extraordinary combination.

Like Liz.

He leaned against the door frame and folded his arms over his chest, taking serious notice of the woman who'd morphed from the girl he'd known years ago. Why hadn't he paid more attention to Liz in high school? Why hadn't he recognized her as more than just the quiet, nice girl who had sat behind him in homeroom, who always had a shy smile to offer despite her braces, who had such fabulous doe-brown eyes under her glasses?

A girl who was smart enough to see through his bravado and not give him another look. Back then he was too interested in sports and running for student council and being the guy who was always ready to serve up quick remarks and find encouragement from his entourage of flunkies. What a fool he'd been.

What a bigger fool he had been the day before to turn down Liz's offer to dance with her in the contest.

When Liz finished her exercises at the barre, she picked up the rhythm of the song filling the studio, her feet moving in well-calculated moves, body in sync, shoulders rolling fluidly. With arms outstretched, she leaped once to the right and then turned sharply, stopping short as if she were caught in a snare. Face-to-face with Tyler, her mouth dropped open, and she quickly smoothed down the long gossamer shirt that covered her black leotard.

Tyler, still leaning on the door frame, clapped, the lone beat echoing in the studio.

"Nice of you to knock," Liz sniped, composing herself.

He broke into a wide grin. "That was my original intention, but you were lost in your dance moves. Didn't want to disturb the artiste."

She turned on her toes with a little huff, walked to the stereo, and flicked it off. "Can the *artiste* help you?" she asked, her tone acidic.

Tyler sauntered into the studio, approaching her boldly. "That was quite a dance."

Liz arched her eyebrows. "I didn't think you cared about dancing."

"And I thought you said I was the best male dancer in Olson." He cocked his head and pursed his lips, toying for a response.

Liz shifted and looked toward the floor. "What does that have to do with anything?"

Tyler placed a finger under her chin, lifting her head. "Well, I saw the way you just danced. Quite impressive, Liz Pruitt. Quite impressive indeed. If I'm the dancer you think I am—and I'm not making any promises— I'd say, with you at the helm, we could probably blow away the competition in that contest."

Liz furrowed her brow. "Are you saying you'll dance with me in the contest?"

Tyler nodded while his mouth turned upward into a confident smile.

"Why the change of heart?"

He shrugged. "Chance to win some money. A little fun." He winked. "Beautiful partner. What's not to like about the setup?" He turned away, breaking her stare, then slowly turned back to her.

She folded her arms in front of her chest with a jerk and faced him with an iron stance. "You've never been one to look away, Tyler. Something you want to tell me?"

He tensed. No, he didn't want to tell her. But she was too smart to believe his intentions were totally admirable. And he was too smart to think he could deceive Liz. He had only one choice—to come clean now. "I think we can swing a deal," he said, his voice low.

"Deal?"

"You need a dance partner so you can win this contest, right?"

She nodded.

"Well, if you agree to this deal, and if we dance together and win, you can keep the whole ten grand." Perhaps upping the stakes would tantalize her, convince her she needed him. As it was, the insensitive fool he'd been when they shared a soda on his boat the day before was stupidly reminiscent of the goof she probably remembered from high school. He had his work cut out to show her he wasn't nearly that bad.

Tyler grabbed Liz's hand and tugged her to the chairs on one side of the floor. They sat, and he leaned close to her, so close he could smell the sweet, outdoorsy scent of her perfume and see the hazel flecks in her eyes.

"I'll level with you, Liz. I need some bucks to get my boat fixed, get my charter business going. It's important to me, to the memory of . . . Anyway, my father just dropped this bomb on me about some crazy Augustine Trust my family has."

"Trust?"

"You probably guessed that my family has some money."

She nodded, eyes wide with interest.

"Well, in six months, when I turn thirty, I'll be eligible for a ten thousand dollar advance on my inheritance."

"Sounds like good fortune is coming your way, Tyler," Liz replied. "I'm happy for you, but what does this have to do with the dance contest?" She wrinkled her nose.

Tyler swallowed hard, inhaling to muster his courage. He rarely met a woman who intimidated him. Why was it so important that Liz think well of him? After all, he was just looking for a vehicle to help him secure his trust, not a lifelong friend. "Well, you need me to help you win the dance contest."

"And what's in it for you to help me win the contest if you don't even want the money?" She lowered her head and looked up at him with the top of her eyes.

He took a deep breath. "There's another wacky stipulation to this trust. I have to be married, or well on my way—wedding plans, the whole nine yards—by the time I'm thirty, maybe a few months after that if my father decides to cut me a break, which, quite honestly, would surprise me." He shuffled his feet and twisted in the chair, pulling farther from her. Then he caught her steely gaze and let the words ramble out. "I need you to pretend to be my fiancée."

Liz was silent as his words seeped in; then a laugh

came blurting out. "I didn't know stand-up comedy was part of your repertoire. Silly me to think that all you were was a football star, prom king, and class president."

He reached for her hand, holding it tightly. "I'm not kidding, Liz. I need a fiancée." He leaned in closer. "I need you, Liz." For what seemed much longer than a few seconds, neither spoke. "And you need me too," Tyler added.

"No, I need money to keep this studio open," Liz replied.

He was surprised at how her words stung. And he reminded himself to pay more attention to nice bookworms in his next life. "Okay, then. So let's look at this as a business arrangement. You pretend to be my fiancée, we dance in the contest and win, and we each end up with ten grand in our pockets. Everyone's happy."

"And what about a wedding? Do we have to fake that too? I don't like deceit." She grimaced. "Apparently it doesn't bother everyone."

He held up his hands. "Hold the phone. I wouldn't be getting anything that's not rightfully mine. This trust is just an advance on my inheritance. So what's the difference if I get it in six months or forty years? I figure we could pretend to be engaged, with the wedding scheduled to take place a month after I turn thirty. When I turn thirty, I'll get the money, fix my boat, and get some charters going. Then we'll call off the wedding. In no time, my business will be booming, and I'll be able to pay back the ten thousand to the trust. And you'll have your ten thousand from the contest to boot."

Liz scowled.

"No one gets hurt, and no one steals any money. It's just a little creative financing." He winked and smiled widely. "Think of it. It's a brilliant plan!"

Liz stood. "Find someone else to play your little game, Tyler. I'm not the needy high school girl you seem to think I am."

Tyler jumped to his feet and nodded. She stood just inches shorter than he, so they were almost eye to eye—the perfect height for a dance couple. "I can see that," he said before leaving.

"Are you crazy?" Julie asked Liz. "You had it all sewn up, and you blew it." She bounced her hands off her head.

Sitting on the front-porch steps, Liz perspired from more than just the July heat. Her face felt flushed, almost feverish. "I had to do the right thing," she told her friend, wondering if her voice sounded as whimpery as she felt.

"You mean the *dumb* thing." Julie grabbed Liz's arm and shook it. "Do you remember all those guys you auditioned? Two left feet, three heads. If you think you have any chance at all—any at all—to win that dance contest, you need Tyler Augustine."

"I just don't like the whole secretive air surrounding

this. I won't lie to my mother." Liz flipped her hair up and held it on top of her head to cool her neck.

"Then just tell her. Grace is understanding."

"Now who's the dumb one?" Liz retorted with a snort.

Julie leaned back on the railing, exasperated. "Well, you can't let your mother turn into a vagrant and lose her home and business. Then she'd have to move in with you." She emphasized her statement with a wag of her finger and twist of her lips.

Liz thought for a few moments. She twisted her hands together, searching for something to give her the nudge she needed, playing all sides of the story over and over in her head. Tyler's proposition was way out of her comfort zone. But there was no quicker or better route to get the money to save the studio. And Tyler wasn't really taking what wasn't his, right? He was just going to get it a little earlier than expected, as a loan. That would really help him. And he did deserve to be helped. He'd grown up, matured from that irresponsible teenager she'd known from afar. Over the past couple of weeks, she'd seen some sweetness in him, some genuine goodness. The sensitive grandson still grieving for his grandfather. The man wanting to make a living, find his own way. Yet . . .

"Sure you're not just afraid of Tyler or afraid to *pretend* to be the future Mrs. Tyler Augustine?" asked Julie.

"No, no. Of course not," Liz said adamantly. "What's to be afraid of?" The perfect dimples that sat even deeper in his post-high-school face. The way he related to Rex's runaway moods. His comment about Liz's having been out of his league. No, Tyler didn't scare her at all. The pretending, however, did.

"Enjoying the sun, ladies?" asked Bobby, startling the friends as he approached the top step. "Fine day. Who gets the prize today?" He smiled with a mouth that was a little too wide for his narrow face and held up a stack of mail, mostly envelopes that had the familiar, foreboding cellophane panes.

Julie pointed to Liz without saying a word.

The nudge she needed.

"Looks like you hit the jackpot," joked Bobby, delivering a little wink along with the mail.

"Actually, looks like she'll *need* a jackpot to pay all those bills." Julie arched an eyebrow at Liz.

"I think I found it," said Liz quietly, trembling hand reaching for the stack of bills.

Chapter Eight

"Now, let's get the rules straight," Liz lectured Tyler as she balanced against a wall of his boat, feeling more synchronized with the ripples of the harbor than the first time she had stood on deck.

"Just be careful," he said. "Don't topple backward. The newspaper would have a field day with the story about my fiancée taking a dive into the drink."

Hearing the word *fiancée* coupled with those irresistible dimples and sea blue eyes almost made her forget how nervous this whole arrangement made her. "I'm not your—" she began and then caught herself, realizing that, in name anyway, she was indeed his fiancée. A title, she guessed, she wouldn't have much trouble getting used to in another context.

"So we're in agreement," Liz began. "In exchange

for dancing in the contest with me, I'll pretend to be your fiancée for six months, until you turn thirty. Then . . ."

"When do you turn thirty? Guess I should know my fiancée's birthday," Tyler said, his tone playful. He tossed a red and white fishing bobber into the air and caught it with a quick snatch of an outstretched hand.

"In eight months," Liz said. "Now, can we concentrate on—"

"Well, this *engagement* comes in handy for you too." He smirked. "Don't girls want to snag a guy by the time they're thirty?"

Liz stood up straight and met him with a scowl. "Get out of the Dark Ages, Tyler. A woman doesn't need a man—at any age. Sometimes a girl is better off alone."

He reached up and tugged her hair. "And sometimes not. Not everyone is meant to be alone, you know."

She exhaled and rolled her eyes. "Now, can we please get serious here? When you turn thirty, you get your ten thousand dollars from the trust, and when we win the dance contest, I get to keep the ten thousand dollar prize, right?"

"That's the deal," he said. "Want to put it in writing?"

"No. I trust you," she said without hesitation. She was startled to hear her own words spoken with such certainty. She really did trust him, although he hadn't done anything in particular to win that trust. A gut reaction, perhaps?

"And you promise, *promise,* to pay back the trust when your business is up and running?" She twisted her fingers into a knot and held them close to her mouth, begging for the answer that was so important to her.

He held up two fingers to mimic the Boy Scouts pledge. "You have my word." He looked at her intently, his expression softening, filling with concern. He reached out and placed a hand on her shoulder. "You're one stand-up girl, Liz Pruitt. No matter what you ever thought of me, what distorted hotshot, teenage rumors ever bounced around your head about me, you have to believe I will give back every penny to the trust. I know that's important to you, and you have my word. Believe me?"

Liz nodded.

"I'd never do anything to compromise the memory of my grandfather or the show of faith you've given me," he said. "We've known each other a long time, Liz."

"Not really, Tyler," she replied. "I thought I had figured out the enigma years ago, but I can only guess at who you are now."

"Look, Liz," he began. "My father and I never had the closest relationship. He's a good man, but he retreated into a shell when my mother died twenty-five years ago. Guess I can't blame him. But my grandfather came to be the male role model in my life. He was the one who always made me feel special, who shared his time with me. The one thing we loved more than anything was to spend a lazy Saturday on the water, fishing, talking. He knew my secrets and dreams. He shaped my life. He encouraged me to see the world, follow my heart's desire. I miss him so much. That's why I want to have a prosperous charter business. To fish this magnificent lake in his memory. So when he looks down from heaven, he sees I really did turn out to be the man he always knew I could become." Tyler's eyes became glassy, and he turned his head away. "I've never shared that with anyone. No one but you, Liz." His voice was laced with embarrassment.

She smiled slightly, touched at his openness.

"Hope you're not disappointed."

Disappointed? On the contrary, she was thrilled. Tyler's words gave her the chance to peel back those layers of youthful bravado and see the real man. He wasn't all spit and vinegar, the cocky boy with the gorgeous face and overabundance of charm. Tyler was a good man who needed to heal his grief and find himself. She could help him do that.

"Uh," Liz began and then hesitated. "What if we don't win?"

"Liz, let's just concentrate on winning. With you as my teacher, we'll be the ones to beat. Now, don't slip back into that mousy high-school persona. A little confidence, please. Give those dazzling, long legs of yours the credit they deserve for once!"

Tyler was right. She had to be positive, had to think and act like a winner. Easier said than done for the girl who'd been raised in the shadow of the great Grace Pruitt.

"Oh, yeah, I almost forgot." Tyler pulled a small

black velvet box from his shirt pocket and handed it to Liz. "We have to do this right."

She looked at him with suspicion and opened the box. Inside was a glassy stone—she guessed it was about two carats—set in a silvery metal, glittering like a beacon under the dusky light. Her mouth gaped open. He really had given this charade some thought. "This is a great-looking fake."

"Fake? Tyler Augustine would never give his fiancée a fake!" he said with mock disdain.

"Stop kidding," Liz shot back, her eyes still glued to the jewel.

"I'm not kidding. It's as real as that astonished look on your face. It was my mother's. I know this is just a six-month loan, but we may as well do it up right, don't you think?"

She looked from the ring to Tyler and back to the ring. Suddenly this all seemed a little too real. His mother's ring? What kind of guy lent a girl he barely knew a huge diamond—a family heirloom, no less—to play a game?

The real question was, what kind of girl accepted?

"So that's the story, Mom." Liz poured herself a second bowl of cereal as she and Grace finished eating breakfast at the kitchen table.

"I don't approve of deception," Grace said softly, her eyes smoldering with a controlled, familiar fire. "I don't want to die knowing that my daughter sold her soul."

Grace had been silent while Liz relayed the details of the dance contest, the Augustine Trust, and her fake engagement to Tyler. She could see her mother's agitation increase as Grace realized she had no control over this situation. Liz didn't want to be disrespectful, but this was no time for her to coddle her mother, soothe Grace's fragile ego. She had a huge task to accomplish, and she had to concentrate all of her efforts into making this work. Now wasn't the time to mince words or spare feelings. It had taken her a sleepless night and some deep soul-searching to come to grips with the situation herself. Grace was on her own to accept it.

"First of all, you're perfectly healthy, so cut the grim-reaper talk. You also don't approve of losing your business and home," Liz said pointedly. "You've worked too hard for all of this, Mom. I made a promise to myself to help you out the best I can. Now you have to make a promise to let me do what I have to do."

Grace pursed her lips, nodded slightly, reached for the crutches leaning against the counter, and hobbled out of the room.

Liz had won round one.

"I've been taking care of you and this house for twenty-five years," Agnes said to Tyler. "And I have to say, this just may be the craziest thing I've heard in all that time." She kneaded the pie dough on the floured countertop, her heavy arms and strong hands flattening and re-rolling the dough several times.

Tyler jumped up backward onto the counter next to her, legs dangling as he swigged from a bottle of grape juice. "No choice."

"You father isn't going to be happy if he finds out about your little scheme," Agnes added. She sprinkled more flour onto the ball of dough and continued to knead it.

"So you don't think this will work?"

"Honey, I didn't say it wasn't a brilliant plan. It's just crazy, that's all. I always thought the Augustine Trust was a ridiculous setup. My great-great-aunt worked for Max, and family legend has it that the old codger was as crazy as a loon. Imagine trying to preserve the bloodline by insisting your heirs be married by the time they're thirty. High time someone squashed that stupid notion." She brushed a curl from her forehead with the back of her wrist, leaving a smudge of flour.

"So you won't tell Dad?" Tyler drained the bottle.

"Well, if I didn't tell him about the time you turned your mother's silver teapot into a tank for pollywogs, mixed his imported pipe tobacco with mud for your Indian village model, or snipped his prize roses to give to that fifth-grade teacher you had a crush on, you can bet I sure won't tell him about this." She winked.

"I knew I could count on you." Tyler reached over to pat her shoulder.

"I can only imagine how desperate poor little Liz Pruitt must feel if she let you rope her into this hare-brained plan. Don't let that little darling get hurt." Agnes raised a floury finger at Tyler.

"I'll take good care of Liz." Tyler jumped down from the countertop. "You have my word on that."

Chapter Nine

Liz and Julie entered the living room as Grace was hanging up the phone.

" 'Morning, Mrs. Pruitt," said Julie, offering her a plate of warm, blueberry muffins. "Just made these, so I wanted to run them over on my way to the restaurant."

Grace reached for one. "They look wonderful, dear." She held the muffin to her nose and took a deep breath. "Heavenly. If I weren't dieting, you know, because of my inactivity, I'd love to try one."

Liz rolled her eyes at her mother's comment. "Who was on the phone?"

"Rita Henshaw, Sam Augustine's secretary." Grace stiffened and pursed her lips. "She called to congratulate me on your engagement to Tyler."

"Oh." Liz looked away from her mother's accusatory stare.

" 'Oh'? Is that all you have to say?" Grace arched her pencil-thin eyebrows, leaving them suspended for what seemed like a very long time.

"Well, we're bound to hear such things," Liz said. "What did you say to Rita?"

"What could I say? That my daughter had fabricated an elaborate plot to keep her mother out of bankruptcy? I just thanked her for her kind words."

"So, that's taken care of," said Liz with a little smile, brushing together her hands as if to sweep the whole incident under the rug.

"Until the next person phones," Grace retorted. "One lie always begets another." She wrapped her arms around herself and shivered.

"Mom, it's not a lie. It's an . . . an arrangement or, rather, a *re*arrangement of things. No one will get hurt."

"Oh, no? How about Sam Augustine? He'll be crushed to find out his son won't end up married to a girl as wonderful as you." Her eyes flashed to Liz.

Liz's mouth gaped open as her mother's gaze locked on her. A girl as wonderful as her? Did her mother really say those words? Liz turned to Julie to find another stunned expression. For a moment, the room was silent.

"I have to go to the studio," Liz finally said to Grace as she turned and hurried out the door, Julie following her.

*   *   *

Liz strapped on her dance shoes and walked around the perimeter of the dance floor, her head down and her hands clasped behind her back. "I can't go through with this," she said to Julie, who sat on the desk, white chef's uniform showing a small blueberry stain on the right sleeve. "My mother just called me *wonderful*. You heard it. *Wonderful*. Well, *wonderful* women don't dream up elaborate plans to bail themselves out of tough situations."

Julie laughed, causing Liz to stop and look at her. "But wonderful women do twist and mold their resources to take care of the people they love. To take care of their mothers. And anyone else they may love." Julie winked at her.

"I don't want to hurt anyone." Liz closed her eyes and raised her hands to her face.

"Well, the only one you're hurting right now is yourself," said Julie. "You win the contest, and Tyler gets an advance on his trust, grows his fishing business to honor his grandfather, and then pays back his father. All is well save a broken engagement that wasn't meant to be anyway. You and Tyler part, and that's that." She snapped her fingers. "Done deal."

Liz pursed her lips. "I guess that is that."

"Look, Tyler is due to show up for practice, and I have to run to the restaurant. Just have fun. For once in your life, *just have fun.*"

A minute after Julie left, Tyler showed up. He stood

in the open doorway, arms crossed, not saying a word. He looked around the studio, sizing up the gleaming hardwood floor and mirrored walls. He didn't look like the cocky, self-assured teenager Liz once knew or the party boy she'd seen at the festival. Clad in jeans and a plain green T-shirt, dwarfed by the high ceilings, and surrounded in the glow from the sun bouncing off the mirrors, he looked almost . . . ordinary. Who was this guy? And where was Tyler the legend?

"Come in," Liz said when he didn't move.

Tyler moved slowly toward Liz in the center of the room. He smiled a big, toothy grin, then slapped his hands on his sides. "So, here we are."

Liz nodded, smiled, and jumped right into business. "We'll dance to 'It's De-Lovely' by Cole Porter. I used this song for my auditions. It's a nice, clean rhythm. Not too fast or too slow. A lot of people know it, so it has crowd appeal. That's important for a contest. Let's listen." She walked to the stereo and flipped it on, letting the song filter through the studio, shaking off memories of the ill-fated auditions.

While Tyler listened, he moved casually, taking in the song, feeling the beat. She was impressed at the way he moved, even absentmindedly, with the music. She became encouraged that they would be able to dance well to the song, please the audience, and, with any luck, impress the judges. Suddenly the chance to win the contest glimmered on her horizon.

"Cool tune," said Tyler when the song ended. "Old-fashioned but cool. Seems to me I remember my grandfather listening to it years ago. Oh, before I forget, we need to make plans for you to come for dinner. My father wants to meet my, uh, fiancée." He winked.

Liz fought to keep her composure. Of course Tyler's father would want to meet her. Why hadn't she considered that? Sam Augustine was one of the most successful businessmen in town. He was the epitome of social grace and decorum. He had probably told his business cronies about the engagement, his son's future. . . .

"Oh, yeah, uh, sure," Liz stammered, wondering just how long she could delay the dinner.

"By the way, you look really nice with your hair pinned up." He perused her head and nodded approvingly. "Very sophisticated and classy. All grown-up."

Liz felt her cheeks color. A compliment from a handsome man had always made her blush, but this one little comment from her fake fiancé was enough to turn up the heat and make her burst into flames.

"Let's try this." She raised her arms to Tyler. "Just follow my steps the best you can."

Tyler placed his arms around her, and they moved slowly to the fox-trot steps. One, two, three, four, sliding their feet together on the fourth count. Over and over again they repeated the simple pattern until they had circled the dance floor.

"Good job," said Liz after they made one rotation.

"Let me put on the music, and we'll try it again. Just take it slowly at first until you get comfortable."

Pushed by the easy swing of the song, they again circulated around the room, familiarizing themselves with the feel of each other, the notion of holding each other in their arms, establishing that all-so-important sense of trust and confidence that dance partners—any partners, for that matter—need to have. Liz smiled. "Keep going." She pushed Tyler a little faster, adding a small hop to her step, which he easily imitated.

Tyler laughed. "Okay, okay. So this is fun. You're a good teacher, Liz."

"Keep going," she instructed. "Stop looking in the mirror and thinking about the steps. Pretend it's just us, dancing for fun, not trying to win a contest. Just think of the art of the dance, and let your feet take over."

When the music stopped, they gave each other a high five.

"Now, that's the way to dance." Tyler's voice dripped with excitement. "Like we've been doing it for years."

"Nice job," said Liz, beaming. She'd expected to find success with Tyler's dancing, but she was genuinely surprised at how well he did, at how well they did together. "Want to try it again?"

Tyler looked at his watch. "Maybe just one more time. I have to get going soon."

"Already?"

He raised his eyes. "Well, I met this woman at the gas station yesterday, and we kind of have, uh, a date."

Liz dropped her head and bore a hold through him with her eyes. "A *date*?"

"Kind of. Just meeting at the coffee shop."

"But you can't have a date. You're engaged. To me!"

He raised his hands. "I know, but technically not . . ."

"But everyone *thinks* we're engaged. It's bad enough to be roped into a fake engagement. I sure don't want to be 'engaged' to a two-timer!" Her voice was louder than it needed to be.

"Hey, I didn't mean . . . Look, I'm sorry." He raised his hands in surrender.

"No, I'm the one who's sorry. Just go!"

"Hello," said Liz, answering the phone on her way through the kitchen.

"May I speak with Grace Pruitt?" asked the businesslike voice on the line.

"She's sleeping," said Liz. "This is her daughter. May I take a message?"

The woman cleared her voice before speaking. "Would you ask your mother to call Fletcher's Appliances about a payment she sent recently for her dishwasher?"

Liz closed her eyes and felt the blood drain from her head. "Did the check bounce?" she asked flatly.

"Well, uh, I guess since you're her daughter, I can say. Yes, yes, it did bounce," the woman replied, her tone a bit softer.

Liz sighed. "I do apologize. I'll give my mother the message, and we'll be sure to send a replacement check right away." Liz calculated in her head that payments for this week's dance classes would be due in a few days. She should be able to send a payment to Fletcher's from that money.

When she hung up the phone, Liz pounded her fist on the countertop. "Mother," she groaned quietly to the empty room. "Why didn't you study finance instead of dance? Ugh! I'll never find another partner for this contest." *Certainly not one who feels so right when we're dancing. Certainly not one who just feels so right.*

"Let me know how you like the cinnamon rolls." Julie set a foil-covered plate on the desk and turned to leave the studio.

"I already know I love them," replied Liz, not stopping her warm-up at the barre while she inhaled deeply the sweet, spicy aroma. She reached forward and bent at the waist into a perfect right angle. "But I don't love the extra pounds I'll gain by eating them all."

"Now you sound like your mother," Julie retorted.

"If that's a challenge to eat every roll, I accept." Liz bent to touch the floor with open palms and stretched as high overhead as her arms would allow.

"Live a little," said Julie with a quick wiggle of her fingers. "Everyone needs a treat now and then. I'll give you a call tonight."

Julie opened the studio door to leave and found herself eye to chest with the mailman, his fist poised to knock.

"Sorry, miss," said Bobby, looking down at Julie.

"Almost used your head as the door knocker." He blushed.

Julie raised her eyes to him. "Uh, my fault for not paying attention and for being only five-three. No harm done." She broke into a wide smile.

"Come on in, Bobby," called Liz from the barre.

"Hi, Liz," said Bobby. He held up a stack of mail. "Too big for your mailbox. Where do you want these?" he asked as he entered the studio, a smiling Julie trailing behind him, apparently sidestepping her plan to leave for work.

Liz recognized the long, slender white envelopes dominating the stack of mail in Bobby's hand. "Just throw them onto the desk," she said, wrenching her face in disgust. "Next to that plate."

Julie trotted to the desk and uncovered the cinnamon rolls, gesturing to them. "Hungry?" she asked Bobby.

Bobby's face lit up when he gazed at the puffy rolls dripping with melted cinnamon-sugar and sprinkled with chopped walnuts. "I am now."

Julie pulled a napkin from the top drawer of the desk and placed a roll on it, handing it proudly to Bobby. "Made them myself just a half hour ago. Still warm."

Bobby accepted the roll with a nod. "You sure know how to put a smile on a guy's face." He took a hearty bite and closed his eyes, displaying exaggerated delight with the pastry. "Mmm, mmm." He wiped a drop of cinnamon from the corner of his mouth. "Something this good should be outlawed. You are magical," he said to Julie, his mouth full.

"No, she's Julie," Liz interjected, straightening up and joining the pair at the desk. Unable to resist any longer, she picked up a roll and took a bite. "Okay, so you're a little bit magical," she joked with her friend, licking the sugar from her lips. "This is amazing, Jule." She took another bite.

Bobby took another hearty mouthful. "Now that these magical rolls have put me into a trance, your wish is my command," he teased Julie. "You name it, and I'll do it."

Julie smiled, pushed spiky tendrils of blond hair behind her ears, and smoothed her white chef's uniform, swishing from side to side. "Careful what you promise," she mocked.

Bobby's gray-green eyes opened widely, sparkling within his narrow face as he pushed the last bite of the cinnamon roll into his mouth. "Whatever your wish is, it's a small price to pay for these rolls."

Julie broke into a mischievous expression, as if she couldn't wait to reveal a secret. Her eyes bounced from Bobby to Liz and back to Bobby. "Dance."

"Huh?" asked Bobby.

"Dance," said Julie. "With Liz."

Liz rolled her eyes and inhaled deeply. "Julie, I don't think—"

"Dance with Liz," Julie said again to Bobby, interrupting her friend. "She needs a partner for a contest—a very important contest."

"A contest?" Bobby furrowed his brow.

"If we win, you'll get five thousand dollars," Liz interjected, sizing up Bobby's tall stature and broad shoulders. Judging from appearances, he might make a good partner. The right tuxedo, a little gel to swish his reddish, stick-straight hair out of his eyes, and a touch of rouge on his pale cheeks, and he might just look the part. She didn't recall his ever tripping over the steps when he delivered the mail. Perhaps Julie's suggestion wasn't too crazy after all. Plus, she was desperate. The only hope she had of entering the contest was to transform Bobby into a viable partner. Now, winning . . . that was another thing.

"And all the cinnamon rolls you can eat," Julie added quickly.

Bobby thought for a second and raised his hands. "You're the last stop on my route. I'm done for the day, so let's get started."

"Just one more time, and we'll call it a day, Bobby." Liz raised her foot to rub the toe he'd stepped on at least a dozen times since they'd started dancing an hour before.

She turned on the music, and she and Bobby plodded through some basic steps. Trying not to grimace after Bobby's big foot stepped on her toes again, Liz told herself that he at least remembered the moves—even if getting him to do them with some flair was like trying to make rain fall upward. She had to give him an A for effort. And he was a willing and cooperative partner. Which was more than she could say for Tyler.

Bobby wrinkled his forehead in concentration and moved his lips as he counted to himself and watched his feet.

"Look into my eyes, and think about the steps," Liz said gently, feeling his body stiffen in her arms. "You're doing well, Bobby. Just *picture* your feet making the right moves while you look up. Eyes on me." She wondered how he'd ever be able to lead her across the floor, as the man needed to do. She could barely get him to loosen up enough to move.

"I've never really danced before," said Bobby. "It's hard to count the steps, remember the moves, and not step on your feet. Sorry, Liz."

"That's okay, Bobby," Liz replied, feeling her big toe throb from the last pummeling Bobby had innocently delivered. If she could shape him into a dancer, she'd at least have a crack at winning the contest. Right now, Bobby was her only hope. He had light-years to go before he came close to being Tyler—in many ways—but Liz was determined to always make the best of whatever the situation presented. She almost believed she could do the same now.

Bobby, a look of deep concentration lining his face, periodically smiled at Liz between counts. She nodded back and kept going. He appeared to be interested and willing to persevere; she was determined to teach him to dance, even if she'd lost track of how many times the song had played.

Rex barked in the backyard. Since Liz wasn't expecting anyone, she guessed the poor dog couldn't stand to listen to the song one more time either and was barking from the strain on his furry little ears. *Be patient, Rex,* she thought. *If I win this contest, I'll buy you all the dog biscuits you can eat.*

"How am I doing, Liz?" Bobby bit his lip as he focused.

His hopeful look tugged at Liz's heart. She'd never lie, but she also wouldn't wound the spirit of a man with so much fortitude. "A girl couldn't ask for a more caring partner. You're really special."

"Really special? More caring partner?" Tyler asked in a whisper as he peered into the studio window, keeping himself hidden from Liz's view. "What's she saying to that dude?" Tyler asked himself, not really expecting an answer and surprised at the degree of agitation he felt.

Rex barked and furiously wagged his tail, standing on his hind legs and stretching his head to the top of the fence.

"Good boy, Rex," said Tyler in a low voice, motioning to the dog to be quiet.

Tyler returned his attention to inside the studio,

grimacing as he watched Liz and Bobby move around the dance floor. "She can't be serious," he whispered, the sound of his voice eliciting a playful yip from Rex.

Tyler noticed the auburn highlights in Liz's hair glistening when they caught the sun as she passed by a window. Her long, shapely legs seemed endless in her black tights, a sharp contrast to the gleaming white of her thousand-watt smile. She stood tall and confident in her silver heels, as if she'd been born to dance. As if she was in exactly the place she was destined to be in. He thought of her in high school, the quiet bookworm sitting behind him in homeroom, offering a shy smile when he bothered to acknowledge she was even in the room. Back then he had been more concerned with impressing his buddies with his audacity than in being a gentleman to the school's best-kept secret. If the last several years and his grandfather's passing had taught him anything, they'd shown him not to waste time, not to let opportunity pass by. Time for Tyler Augustine to grow up.

Tyler crossed his arms over his chest and twisted his face in disgust. "Come on, Liz. You're really dancing with that guy?" He ducked back as Liz and Bobby neared the window, then quickly took another peek and shook his head. "You can do better than that."

Rex whimpered, and Tyler turned to the dog, who looked hopeful that he'd soon be the recipient of some attention. "Liz is *my* partner," he said to Rex, who cocked his head and lifted one ear as Tyler pointed to himself. "She dances with *me*."

Chapter Ten

"Mrs. Pruitt?" Tyler asked when Grace opened the door, balancing on her crutches, clutching a poetry book. He'd never met Liz's mother before, but he saw the resemblance.

"Yes." Her face showed no expression.

"I'm Tyler Augustine." He smiled, hoping for a smile in response.

"I know who you are," Grace replied flatly.

Tyler shifted his weight, leaned against the door frame, and then straightened again. He wondered how she'd recognized him. Then again, mothers had always seemed to know who he was, as if they were always watching him, keeping a wary eye on him. "Is Liz home?"

Grace glared at him. "It's ten o'clock in the evening."

"Yeah, sorry about that. It's just that . . . that I need to talk to her." He waited for Grace to speak. Nothing. "I need to explain . . ."

"She's in the studio," Grace replied.

Tyler turned to retreat down the steps and around the side of the house to the outside studio entrance. "Use the door off the kitchen. Straight through there." Grace pointed.

Tyler nodded and started through the house. The interior was artful and stark, stylishly cold. Decorated in shades of gray and white with a few carefully placed splashes of red and purple, the house looked and felt like an art gallery. Hardwood floors, sparse decorations, and metal accessories accented the roomy interior. The furniture was hard-looking and straight. The home looked like Grace: erect, severe, understated, but aloofly elegant. A look that didn't welcome but that captivated once it engaged you. This didn't look or feel like a home Liz belonged in or was part of. She exuded color—he pictured patchwork quilts, fuzzy throw pillows, and whimsical knickknacks. He wondered if the house had had this austere style when Liz was growing up in it and if she had made her own room a little haven with her signature style.

The door leading from the kitchen into the dance studio was open. Tyler stood in the doorway and watched Liz stretch and run through some steps, soft music reminiscent of a grand ballet emanating throughout the room, creating an ethereal atmosphere in the studio. He'd never seen her dance ballet before, and she was captivating. The peppy, jazzy steps of ballroom were a stark contrast to the nimble elegance of the ballet steps she performed.

After a few minutes, she must have sensed someone's presence, because she turned abruptly to him, her eyes wide with surprise, mouth slightly open.

"Is it too late to practice?" Tyler approached her, hoping she saw the fire and conviction in his eyes. The look was meant to burn that other guy out of her mind, make her forget she'd spent the afternoon in the arms of another man.

She stood stiffly while he neared. "Not another date tonight? Interrupting your dating streak could damage that famous reputation," she sniped.

"No date," he said. "I . . . I thought about what you said. You were right, Liz. If we're supposed to be engaged, I can't be seen with anyone else. I canceled my date."

"So you're here by default," she quipped. "For lack of something better to do."

He forced a little grin. "No, I'm here because I want to be. I want to win this contest."

She arched her eyebrows as if she didn't believe him and was awaiting further explanation.

"Don't dance with that other guy, Liz. I'm the only partner for you."

Liz walked to the stereo and flicked it off with a slap of her hand. She pursed her lips and turned angrily to Tyler. "So *that* explains what Rex was barking at."

"What?"

"This afternoon. Rex only barks at intruders and rodents."

"And which one was I?" asked Tyler with a chuckle.

"Don't make me tell you," snapped Liz. She huffed and crossed her arms. "What were you doing here? Spying on me?"

Tyler forced another smile. "Well, I guess that puts me into the intruder category. Better than a four-legged visitor."

"Don't be so sure," Liz hissed.

His expression went blank, and his voice deepened with seriousness. "Look, Liz, I came here to talk to you, and I found you with . . . with that guy." He crossed his arms over his chest and squared his stance, as if facing off. "You sure didn't waste any time replacing me."

Liz put her head back and laughed, her voice echoing in the studio. "If I hadn't spent two days racking my brain about how I can get some fast cash and wearing my finger to a nub on the calculator as I added up all the bills my mother owes, I'd tell you to take your—"

"He's not good enough for you, Liz." Tyler wasn't backing down.

"Ha! And you are?" The words spewed from her mouth, high and sharp.

"We both know the answer to that," said Tyler with a cocky grin.

Liz bristled. "Why, I should just tell you—"

Tyler placed a gentle hand over her mouth. He placed

the other hand on her shoulder, looking deep into her eyes. "Forgive me?"

Liz watched him for what seemed like a very long time, his hand still on her mouth. She looked into his eyes, searching for the Tyler she'd come to believe existed. Looking for the man who had poured out his heart to her. She found him and nodded.

"Dance with me?" he asked.

She nodded again, her eyes opening wider.

He slid his hands down her arms, grasping her limp hands. "We both know a winning team has to have good chemistry. So let's start fresh. Okay? Let's start over from this minute and do this the way it was meant to be done."

Liz narrowed her eyes, saying nothing, as she walked to the stereo and turned it on. She studied him once again before speaking. "Just follow my lead." Her voice was quiet and hesitant as she poised her arms for his embrace.

"Exactly what I plan to do," Tyler replied with a wink.

"You do dance divinely, Miss Pruitt," Tyler quipped with a southern drawl as they circled the dance floor. "Just divinely." He released his grip on one hand and twirled her under his arm. "You certainly are light on those little feet."

"Big feet," said Liz as they again joined arms. "Size ten monsters. Badly bruised, I might add." Still annoyed with the date he'd almost had—and irritated at herself for caring—Liz managed a halfhearted scowl. "Be careful, or I'll step on you."

Tyler laughed, linked his arm with hers, and circled in a do-si-do spin, while Liz's head rotated in an attempt to follow him. He again pulled her close and continued their dance.

"Enough goofing around," she said, unable to sound angry at his antics. "Concentrate on the steps." She was impressed that even their banter and his silliness didn't interfere with Tyler's ability to stay on tempo. Did this guy ever miss a beat? In dance or in life?

"Try this." Liz interjected a new step, testing Tyler's uncanny comfort on the dance floor. She turned her back to him, reached backward for his hands, and placed them on her hips. She moved left, then right. "Don't lose the rhythm," she cautioned. "Concentrate. One, two, three—"

"Together," Tyler said, finishing her count. He spun her to face him and pulled her a little more closely than the dance required.

When the song ended, they both crumpled to the floor, exhausted. He sat with one knee elevated, arm resting on it. "We're good." He waggled his eyebrows. "Really—good."

"Don't get too smug." Liz wagged a finger at him. "Just because we had a good session, even with the unconventional steps you improvised, doesn't mean we don't have a lot of work still to do. We're just starting to . . . to get . . . the feel of each other." She felt her face flush, hoping he wouldn't misinterpret the innocent intention of her words. Of course, he wouldn't. Tyler didn't think of her in those terms. He was a man on a mission: a mission to pull off a charade and get a few bucks. Romance was most certainly the last thing on his mind.

Tyler didn't flinch. "Come on. Admit it. We really are off to a good start." He stretched out his leg to nudge her foot with his.

"I suppose," Liz admitted reluctantly.

Tyler studied her. "You know what your problem is, Liz? You're afraid to have fun. You know we can blow away the competition. If you loosen up, that is."

She gasped. "You have a lot of nerve critiquing me, Tyler. Who's the dancer here anyway?" She placed her hands on her hips with a quick flick and tightened her lips into a slit.

He held up his hands in surrender. "Hey, I'm just saying you need to have more fun. Don't be so afraid to have a good time."

"I *am* having fun." Liz didn't crack a smile. "I'm not one of those giggly, bubbleheaded girls you always dated. Or someone who'd meet you in a gas station one day and agree to date you the next."

Tyler's lips twisted with amusement. "At least you don't hold a grudge." He jumped to his feet and pulled Liz to hers with an easy tug.

She wanted to stuff the words back into her mouth, pull a sheet over her head, and hide in plain sight. She sounded like a jealous child, pouting because she almost didn't get her way. Almost. After all, Tyler was here with her. For whatever that was worth. Technically, she'd won, although she wasn't sure what she'd won. "Look, Tyler. Don't confuse things here," Liz said quietly. "I know everything about this arrangement is just for convenience, for both of us. In a few months we'll part company, and you can go back to doing your thing, whatever that is, with whomever you want to do it. And I'll go back to—"

"Taking care of your mother, running after your dog, and not having much fun," Tyler interjected, wiggling his nose at her like a rabbit.

"That's not true." Liz knew her tone was more defensive and less convincing than it needed to be.

He chuckled. "Well, if you don't want to have fun after this contest is over, there's not much I can do about that. But while you're my fiancée . . ."

Liz inhaled deeply and caught her breath. Her lungs felt deflated, unable to hold even a mouthful of air. Must Tyler refer to her as his fiancée? She'd been looking for a dance partner, not a future husband. And she surely didn't want it to appear she'd found a future husband when it was all a sham. The title of fiancée was reserved for the lucky woman Tyler chose for real, not the figment of what it could be. "When the contest is over, with any luck, we'll have a few good memories—nothing more."

Tyler smirked. "I'd say we're already past that." The smile disappeared from his face, replaced by an air of seriousness, determination. He grabbed her into his arms and led her around the floor, repeating the steps they'd done just minutes before. They moved in perfect rhythm, no music necessary to keep them in sync. She felt him sense her steps, as if he could read her mind, as if they were one. No longer were Liz and Tyler separate dancers—at that moment they became partners, anticipating the other's moves, sensing the other's mood. The dance had become them—and together they became the dance.

After they circled the floor several times, he stopped, jolting her to a quick halt. Tyler looked at Liz intently. "There's one for the memory book."

From the corner of her eye, Liz saw Grace in the doorway. Liz had been so consumed by the dance, by Tyler's transformation, she hadn't even noticed Grace. And she didn't want her mother to infringe on this moment, to steal a bit of the emotion that Liz would, no doubt, have to call on when she and Tyler were a thing of the past. With a sigh, Liz turned toward her mother.

Grace's expression was stoic, probing, shadowed in the darkened doorway. "Be warned," she said to Liz and Tyler. "A well-executed dance, as you just performed, will change your lives forever."

Chapter Eleven

"Hope that wasn't a problem—my coming over here so late last night." Tyler laced on the new dance shoes Liz had found in the tiny closet of dance products Grace kept at the studio. A piece of missing inventory certainly wouldn't make a difference to the studio's financial troubles. "Your mother didn't act too happy to see me." He stood and flexed his feet in the new shoes, then grimaced.

"Oh, that *was* her happy face." Liz purposely injected sarcasm into her tone. "That's about as smiley as she gets." She shrugged.

Tyler walked gingerly in the new shoes, then jumped straight up a few times as if he was on a pogo stick. "Even without the smile, she's a beautiful woman. Stunning." He looked at Liz. "Runs in the family."

Liz eked out a small grin, trying to hide her surprise at his comment.

"Good to see you smile. A smile is like a spotlight on a gorgeous face."

Now whose face was he talking about? Liz knew that her mother was the striking beauty in the family. *Gorgeous* had never been a word Liz had pinned on herself.

"How do the shoes feel?" Liz preferred to focus on feet rather than faces. Much safer.

Tyler ran, literally ran, across the floor, coming to a sliding skid at the other end of the studio. He repeated the movement back across the floor, landing nose to nose with Liz. He stuck a finger into the side of one shoe, feeling the tightness. "A little snug, but not bad."

"They'll loosen up as you wear them." She bent and felt the toe of his shoe. "Good fit. They look really nice."

"Black patent leather? I don't know about looking *nice*. I just hope they don't look too . . . girly." He glanced down at the highly polished shoes, the reflection from the overhead lights bouncing on the tops.

Liz curled her lips and shook her head. "Believe me, no one will find anything about you girly. Not with your reputation."

Tyler clasped his hands behind his back, raised his nose, and looked at Liz with probing eyes. " 'Reputation'? Just what does that mean?"

"Uh, I . . ." Liz stammered and looked away. When Tyler didn't respond, she turned back to him. He hadn't changed his staunch pose, and his body language clearly said he was anticipating—expecting—a response, although his expression smacked of playfulness.

"I'm waiting," he said softly, his lips turning upward just enough to raise a hint of a dimple.

Liz shuffled a foot at something invisible. Tyler's tone sounded disturbingly like Grace's had when she used to scold Liz. "You know," she started, her mouth dry, "the sports cars, the girls behind the bleachers."

Tyler threw back his head and roared. "Liz, I have a news flash for you." He placed a hand on her arm. "High school boys exaggerate—a lot. I'm sure my *reputation* led a much more interesting life than I did."

"Really?" She wrinkled her brow. She mused over the possibility of Tyler's not being the legend she'd come to believe he had been. Then what?

"Can we please just dance? I have to break in these shoes before they kill me." He took her hand and led her to the middle of the floor, then opened his arms to accept her dance pose. "Yesterday is gone. Today is all that matters."

She inhaled deeply. "Okay, then. Let's start from the beginning. One, two, three—"

"Together," he added quickly.

"Is he gone?" Julie poked her head into the open studio door, moving her big, greenish, curious eyes quickly around the room.

"Left a few minutes ago to run an errand," replied Liz. "He'll be back in an hour."

"Rats," said Julie with a snap of her fingers. She entered the studio and set a take-out bag of food labeled *Crystal Cove* on the desk. "I was hoping to see Dance Guy Extraordinaire in action. How's he doing?" She flashed an exaggerated wink and fanned herself.

"Amazing," said Liz. "He catches on so quickly. His dancing is really fantastic. If he'd been formally trained, there'd be no stopping him."

Julie sat on the edge of the desk and straightened her stained apron. "I didn't ask about his dancing," she said with a sassy grin. "How fantastic is *he*?"

Liz adjusted the tie of the pink dance sweater hugging her waist over her white leotard. "Are you talking about the Tyler of today or the Tyler of yesterday?"

"Huh?"

Liz pulled her hair back, knotted it carelessly, and let it fall over her shoulders. "No matter what way you look at it, Tyler is fantastic. But you know what's weird? He denies having been a reckless high school boy. Can you believe that?"

"Really?" Julie reached into the bag and set white foam containers, paper plates, napkins, and plastic forks on the desk. "Have some lunch while it's hot."

Liz opened a container holding what appeared to be chicken mixed with mushrooms and rice. "Why would he say that? Does he think I'm stupid? That I didn't notice what he was like?" She held the container close to her face and inhaled deeply. "Smells great."

"A new recipe I created." Julie opened another container holding penne pasta under strips of gravy-coated beef. "I call it Chicken Roberto. This is Beef Jules." When a drop of sauce smudged her finger, she licked it off. "Maybe we were wrong about him back then." She took the container of chicken from Liz and dished some onto a paper plate. "Want some beef?"

Liz looked at the pasta and beef. "Chicken Roberto? Very subtle. That pasta looks wonderful, but I can't overdo the carbs."

"People who watch carbs are a chef's nightmare." Julie portioned a hearty helping of the beef and pasta onto her own plate and quickly shoveled some into her mouth. "If I were tiny like you, I'd eat spaghetti, bread, and potatoes every day."

Liz took a forkful of the chicken. She sighed in pleasure as she chewed.

"To scaredy-cat girls like us, all the boys in high school were wild," said Julie, returning to the topic of conversation. She reached into the container of chicken and plopped a hearty forkful onto her plate. She chewed, licked her lips, and shook her head slowly. "Not bad, but it needs more . . . something. Maybe a little nutmeg to give it a nuttier flavor."

Liz took another bite of her lunch. "This is yummy just as it is. Maybe our perception of guys was skewed back then. I mean, what did we know?"

"Maybe our perception was, but our eyes weren't," said Julie with a full mouth. "Tyler was gorgeous then and gorgeous now. There's no denying that."

That word again. When spoken in the context of Tyler, it fit perfectly. "Well, all the 'gorgeous' in the world won't win this dance contest. I just hope we can pull this off." Liz preferred not to let her thoughts and feelings stray from the task at hand. She was knee-deep in some serious business and needed to totally focus on the contest. Even the perfect Tyler Augustine wouldn't get in the way of that.

"Doubts?" Julie wiped her mouth before dishing out another helping of pasta.

"No doubts about the dancing," said Liz with a lift of her eyebrows. "But I'm not so sure about the engagement."

Julie's eyes lit up, and a devilish grin popped onto her face. "So how much fun is it to be engaged to Tyler Augustine?" She batted her eyelashes and dreamily laid a hand on her chest.

Liz stomped a foot. "No fun at all. I don't like the pretending." And she was annoyed at how much time she spent wondering what the real thing would be like. "It makes me uneasy."

"I want to get into baking wedding cakes," said Julie. "You know, maybe open a little bakery off the restaurant. I can bake your cake."

Liz glared at her friend, then tossed her empty paper plate into the trash. "So you bake fake cakes for fake weddings? To feed a fake reception of hundreds of Sam's society friends?" She grimaced and rubbed her temples to ward off the brewing headache.

"The cake topper could be a bride and groom wearing little dance shoes," Julie continued, her tone full of good-natured teasing.

"Argh," said Liz through clenched teeth. "Not funny! There will be no wedding, fake or real!"

Julie cracked a smile. "I wonder what your fiancé would say about that."

Shortly after Julie left for the restaurant, Tyler hurried through the door of the dance studio, a fishing rod over his shoulder. He placed it in front of himself, shook it to check the flexibility, smiled with approval, then leaned it gingerly in a corner. "That's a beauty," he said. "A real beauty."

"What's a beauty?" asked Liz, doing deep knee bends at the barre.

"This fishing rod I ordered from Adirondack Zak's Sport Shop. They called last night to tell me it came in."

"Oh," Liz replied, not really following Tyler's drift and unable to share his enthusiasm for the black graphite stick. "So that's the errand you had to run?"

"Yep. Just look at it. Now there are two beauties in this room."

She stopped abruptly midbend and caught his gaze, trying to extinguish the glow she was sure had lit up her face like the sun. "Is that for your charter business?"

"Sure is. You can never have enough fishing equipment. As soon as my boat is back in operation, a lucky fisherman is going to use that rod to land some of the finest fish that Lake Ontario will give up." He smirked, then raised his nose and sniffed. "What's that smell?"

"Julie stopped in with some food from her restaurant. Too bad you weren't here to enjoy it. I'm sorry there's none left." She felt guilty that she hadn't saved some lunch for Tyler. She turned on the stereo.

Tyler sat in a chair and slipped on his dance shoes. "I grabbed a burger at the diner. Speaking of food, my father keeps asking when my fiancée is coming to dinner."

Liz felt her breath catch, and she stopped cold, still reeling from his referring to her as a beauty, even if she had had to share the limelight with a fishing rod. Tyler had only been in the studio for a few minutes, and already he had her standing on her head. He had a way of doing that. "Dinner?"

"That's what families do," said Tyler. "You know, meet the in-laws. Except the Augustines first have hors d'oeuvres, then dinner, then dessert and coffee. So come hungry. Tomorrow at seven. Dad expects your mom to join us."

"Well . . . I'll . . . I'll see if she's up to it, with her leg." The thought of telling Grace about this event terrified her. The last thing Liz needed was her mother adding gasoline to the fire about to ignite at the Augustine house. "Who else will be there?"

Tyler shrugged, unfazed. "Just your mother, my father, and Agnes, I guess. And, of course, the happy couple," he mocked, pointing back and forth between Liz and himself. "That's us, in case you didn't know."

Liz felt the blood drain from her head as fast as a runaway elevator hitting the ground. "So Agnes is still with your family?" She recalled the heavyset woman who had driven to school following the famous Corvette incident.

"She's the best thing in that house," said Tyler. "If it weren't for all the guidance Agnes gave me after my mother died, I would have been a real troublemaker."

"Thank goodness for Agnes." Liz wondered how much worse Tyler imagined himself capable of having been.

"She was my salvation and the best thing to ever happen to me." He hesitated. "Until now."

Speechless, Liz pulled her hair behind her head, twisting it as she did when she was nervous. She paced across the floor, willing herself to not fall apart. "What should I wear? What should I say?"

Tyler danced over to her, performing the steps of their routine. He grabbed her by the arm, stopping her from pacing. "Look, Liz, everything will be fine. Agnes is cool with our story, so don't worry about her. She'll play along and keep our cover. Dad will make polite conversation, your mother will be lovely, we'll eat, then you'll go home. Everyone will have a perfectly civilized time. Even if they don't, they'll pretend to. That's the Augustine way."

"How will I be able to look your father in the eye? My goodness. I'm pretending to marry his son. How will I be able to act as if everything is normal, as if nothing is wrong?"

Tyler held her hand, entwining his fingers in hers. "You worry too much, Liz. Just be your extraordinary self, and all will be well." He fingered the ring. "And don't forget to wear the rock. It'll all be over before you know it."

"That's what I'm afraid of."

Chapter Twelve

"How interesting that you and Tyler never dated in high school," Sam said to Liz as they sat in the formal parlor of the Augustine home. He reached for another miniature cube of sugar with the small silver tongs, dropped it into his iced tea, stirred, and took a sip. He smacked his lips and nodded with approval. "At least you found each other eventually. I guess things happen in due time."

"True," said Liz, her throat dry, voice shaky. She hadn't felt this uncomfortable since she'd been interviewed by the panel of judges for admittance into the exclusive Oswego Dance Academy for her senior internship at college.

Liz sat at one end of the stiff love seat, Tyler at the other. Her hands lay folded in her lap, resting on a sea of tartan plaid. She'd chosen the most reserved, classic outfit she owned. The pleated, red-plaid skirt; red cardigan, which she'd buttoned almost to her neck over a starched white blouse; and small-heeled black pumps made her look as if she was applying for a librarian's job in the 1950s instead of a woman who should be delighting in the first meeting with her future father-in-law. Her hair was secured by a slim black headband, earrings sat on her lobes like small, silver buttons, and a dainty silver necklace brushed the base of her throat. While she had intended to downplay her jewelry to be in line with her demure outfit, she hadn't intended for her lackluster appearance to accentuate the engagement ring blaring on her left hand like a searchlight. In another situation, she would have adored the ring, been unable to take her eyes off it, found ways to flash it in front of the eyes of envious women. Now the sight of it sent shivers down her spine as it perched boldly on her finger, mocking her pathetic situation and feeling like dead weight.

When Tyler had welcomed Grace and Liz into the house, he had quickly checked Liz's hand for the ring. "Looks good on you," he had whispered into her ear. She was sure he meant that the beautiful bauble would have looked lovely on anyone—despite the low purr in his tone.

Even with her casted leg and crutches, Grace looked elegant in a pencil-thin, below-the-knee, black knit dress and wide leather belt that gave flawless definition to her small waist. A scarf woven with silver thread and black silk looped around her neck and cascaded over one shoulder. On the foot of her uncasted leg, she wore a black ballet slipper. This was Grace's signature style—long, lean, classic. As a child, Liz had often wondered why her mother didn't wear pull-on polyester pants and floral-print blouses that fell loosely over her hips like her friends' mothers did. From her understated elegance to her stoic expression, Grace was as well chiseled as a marble sculpture. She may no longer have been part of the professional stage, but she carried its aura with her wherever she went, an enigma who always seemed to complement whatever environment she found herself in.

And Grace fit perfectly in the Augustine home.

Home was an understatement for the Augustine residence. *Mansion* was a much more accurate tag for the enormous house. It screamed of a place that had harbored a family's fortune for generations. High ceilings, heavy wood trim, large paintings, and elegant decorations accented the impressive parlor. Although the classic furnishings were old, they were in perfect condition, as if they'd always been lovingly cared for. As if they'd actually become better with age. Liz was sure Tyler had never sprawled on these sofas with dirty sneakers or eaten peanut butter sandwiches on these chairs when he was a kid.

"Lovely painting," commented Grace, gesturing to an Impressionistic rendition of ballerinas on stage—a wavy blur of pastel colors, indistinct yet identifiable.

Sam walked to the painting. "My wedding gift to my late wife," he said, adoring eyes on the painting. "She picked it out when we were in Paris for our honeymoon. It was an inexpensive piece from a street vendor, yet she said it had a truth and beauty that you couldn't put a price tag on." His eyes assumed the dreamy haze of a beautiful memory. "Yes, Ellen was the one in the family with an eye for style."

"Very nice," Liz added, feeling some comment was needed.

"Speaking of honeymoons, I guess you two will need to start making plans." Sam turned to Liz and Tyler.

"Someplace with water," Tyler said quickly, grasping Liz's left hand, fingering her ring, and turning to smile at her.

Honeymoon? Liz hadn't given it a thought. She was hoping to make it through the fake engagement and then put this pretense out of its misery. *Someplace with water?* Had Tyler really thought about their fake honeymoon?

"Just a few more minutes and dinner will be ready," said Agnes, walking into the parlor from the kitchen, interrupting the discussion of the honeymoon. She took a seat in the chair next to Grace and smoothed the chiffon apron over her ample lap.

Liz felt dizzy and was sure she'd choke on her meal during dinner. She was so tense, she wouldn't be able to get a morsel down her closed throat. Fake engagements. Fake honeymoons. Even a fake father-in-law who thought he was the real thing. This was all more than her dancing feet ever bargained for.

"So, the mother of the bride must be very busy with wedding preparations," Sam said to Grace. "I certainly hope your broken leg isn't standing in the way of your plans. Agnes will be happy to help."

Grace turned her attention toward Liz, delivering a deadly glance. "Well . . ."

"We need to formulate the guest list," Sam added almost jovially. "I have several business associates I'll have to include. It's most appropriate. And then we'll need an announcement for the society page."

"Sure," Tyler said, not flinching.

Liz almost hyperventilated.

"And where will the reception be held? The country club has a nice facility, or we could even have something catered in our banquet room." Sam looked from Tyler to Liz and back to Tyler.

"We haven't given that much thought," said Tyler, his tone dismissive.

"Now, don't let this wedding go the way of the rest of your life," said Sam, his tone straddling irritation. "Now isn't the time to be happy-go-lucky. A wedding is an important occasion, a big step in someone's life. And an Augustine wedding, well, that's a grand event. It must be planned correctly."

Tyler cleared his throat. "Well, Liz and I are so busy

with our dance contest, we really haven't had time to think about the wedding." His blank expression shot into an abrupt, insincere grin.

Sam's eyebrows slumped into a deep *V*, and he halted the sip of iced tea he was about to take. "Dance contest?"

Liz felt a terrific chill permeate the room, and from the corner of her eye she saw Grace straighten up.

"Well, you know Liz is a dancer, like her lovely mother," said Tyler, passing a charming nod toward Grace, who sat as stiff as ice. Liz wasn't sure if Grace was peeved at being dragged into Tyler's falsehood or at having Liz's inferior dance ability compared to her own.

Sam nodded.

"We decided to enter a ballroom dance contest, you know, for fun."

Liz wondered why Tyler didn't mention the prize money, but perhaps the idea of trying to win money was taboo in this household. Money was to be earned honestly or inherited. Winning was for bingo-playing hacks who hadn't a more dignified way to fill their coffers. Liz gulped. Like her.

"So, I assume this contest is a fund-raiser at that yacht club you go to," said Sam, the question phrased like a statement, as if he'd already made up his mind.

Tyler shook his head. "Actually, no. It's kind of a big deal, sponsored by some outfit that does this around the country. Should be pretty well publicized."

Sam's nostrils flared, and his mouth tightened into a thin line. "That's not usually the type of press our family seeks out." He sounded as if he were trying hard to temper his tone.

"Sorry if you don't approve, Dad, but I hope you'll reconsider and attend the competition. I think Liz and I have a huge chance of winning." He held up her hand in victory, and she wanted to hide under a sofa cushion.

"Perhaps at another time we'll discuss that, but now we should really concentrate on making some wedding plans." Sam pulled the ball back into his court and prepared to take the lead.

"You know, Dad—" Tyler began, his tone defensive.

"Oh, let's not worry about plans tonight," Agnes interrupted. "Everything will fall into place eventually."

Thank goodness for Agnes! Liz was ready to dig into her empty pockets and give the woman her last dime for saving the evening.

"Eventually," Tyler echoed, squeezing Liz's hand a little tighter.

Not in this lifetime, thought Liz.

"Sam Augustine isn't a stupid man," said Grace through clenched teeth as she and Liz drove home after dinner.

Liz said nothing.

"He'll soon figure out this little game you and Tyler are playing." She straightened her collar and smoothed her hair behind her ears. "Then we'll all be deeply embarrassed. Especially Sam, who has his social and business reputation to consider."

If Liz hadn't been driving, she would have shut her eyes and tried to block out all the insanity building in her life. Her mother was worried about being embarrassed when Liz was just hoping Tyler's ruse didn't hold some loophole that would get her thrown into jail.

"Just what do you plan to do about it?" asked Grace pointedly.

Without turning, Liz spoke softly, startling herself with a timbre eerily reminiscent of Grace's scolding tone. "Today three collection letters came in the mail. You have bills to pay, and I made a promise to help make that happen." She turned to Grace. "So this is what I plan to do about it, Mom. I plan to dance."

Liz stood in the middle of the dance floor. Alone. She crossed her arms, tapped the toe of one of her silver heels, pursed her lips, and stared at the clock. 7:25.

Twenty-five minutes late. Way past the pardonable parking-the-car-and-be-right-there late. For twenty-two minutes she had stood there, stewing about Tyler's absence. Her thoughts had run the gamut from detained to accident to careless to inconsiderate brute. Her blood pressure spiked with each solitary moment. Didn't he think she had anything better to do than wait for him? Didn't he realize she had arranged her whole day for their practice? How dare he treat his fiancée so disrespectfully? *Fiancée.* She looked at her hand, at Tyler's ring. She hadn't removed it after they returned from

Tyler's father house last night, even though there was no one around to lead on—except herself.

The clock rang its lonely, single, half-hour chime. "Ugh!" Liz bellowed. She grabbed her purse and car keys and stomped out the door.

As Liz drove into the marina, dusk was starting to settle, and the wet, fishy scent of the heavy night air hovered around her. The tires of her car crunched on the gravel road that paralleled the boardwalk leading to the docks. Her eyes were locked on Tyler's boat as she neared, heart speeding up as the *Fish On* came into focus under the shadow left by the sinking sun.

Tyler was on deck, leaning on the railing, staring at the water. He didn't appear to notice Liz's car or the muffled thud made by the closing of the car door.

She walked quietly to the dock and stood in front of his boat. Her anger had propelled her to this point but had dissipated at the sight of Tyler—standing alone. Not busy with anything that would have caused him to forget practice. Not grease-soaked and elbow deep in a broken engine. And not, thankfully, even occupied with an attractive passerby who had stopped to talk. Just alone.

"Forgive me?" asked Tyler into the night, not turning to Liz.

"How'd you know I was standing here?"

He turned to her. "I'd recognize those footsteps anywhere."

Liz didn't move closer. She waited for him to turn to her, change his posture, act as if he wanted to see her. "You didn't come to the studio, Tyler," she began, holding back the angry words she'd practiced on the drive over. "I . . . I was worried."

"Sorry," he said. "I should have called."

"What's wrong?" Liz asked as concern rippled through her.

He moved to the edge of his boat, forming a dark silhouette against the pinky dusk of the sky. "I can't dance with you anymore, Liz."

Chapter Thirteen

Liz stopped breathing, the air strangled in her tight chest. A strange tingling shot throughout her body, making her feel like an outsider in her own skin, someone witnessing all of this from afar. Had she misunderstood Tyler's words? No, no, she hadn't. The sullen expression on his face reinforced the message.

"You okay?" Tyler inched as far to the edge of the boat as possible.

She took a deep breath, attempted to pull the life back into herself, readied herself. "Fine."

He looked at her through squinted eyes. "You don't look fine."

She knew he was right. Tyler didn't have to tell her that she looked like a wreck. Standing in the warm evening air, pink filmy dance skirt tied around her waist

143

and fluttering in the soft breeze, black leg warmers slouching over silver heels, too-large purse slung over her shoulder, pale skin that no doubt had blanched a few shades lighter upon hearing Tyler's words—no, she couldn't possibly look fine.

Her eyes locked on him. Her mouth opened to speak, but her bottom lip quivered. One tear trickled from her eye, leaving a wavy river of blush in its wake.

Tyler stiffened, alarm clouding his face and mouth gaping open as he focused on the glistening drop running down her cheek. "Liz," he said, voice prickled with apprehension.

She held up a hand to stop him, turned her head, and let the tears escape. She couldn't stop them. Couldn't compose herself. Her emotions were on a roll. She was buckling under the weight of responsibility and loss. No money, no job, no apartment—and now, no Tyler to dance with her.

He jumped over the side of the boat and onto the dock, rushing to Liz, reaching for her. She slipped into the welcoming comfort of his embrace and placed her head on his shoulder. Her weeping continued.

"I hate it when I do things like this." Tyler patted her back as if she were a child.

Liz raised her head and looked at him through watery eyes. "What?" She wiped her eyes with the back of her hand and dug into her purse for a tissue.

"I'm such an idiot when it comes to people's feelings. Now I've made you cry. I'm really sorry, Liz."

"It's not just you, Tyler. It's . . . it's everything." Her shoulders heaved as sobs convulsed her body.

He grinned, and his dimple caught one of the last rays of the day's sunlight. "Other than finding a jerk for a dance partner—one who's even more of a jerk than that mailman—what does a great-looking, talented girl like you have to cry about?"

Liz held up her index finger. "Well, I'm twenty-nine years old and living back home." She held up a second finger. "I gave up my tiny apartment and not-so-profitable job, which both seem opulent right now, to bail out my broke mother—" She held up a third finger, and Tyler interrupted.

He ran his fingers through his hair. "Okay, so this litany could take a while. I have a couple of cold sodas in the fridge. Shall we drown our sorrows?" He grabbed her hand and led her to the boat without waiting for her to agree.

"*Our* sorrows? That's crazy talk. I can't imagine you have too many to drown," Liz said as Tyler jumped onto the boat, held out a hand for her, and hoisted her on board with a quick tug.

Tyler chuckled. "Now who's talking crazy?"

He disappeared down into the galley while Liz sat on the seat overlooking the lake. The August evening was just a bit too perfect to be wasted on self-pity. The large orange sun touched the horizon, dropping lower with each passing second. A few lonely gulls squawked as they circled over the water, taking one last look for a snack before the darkness quieted their hungry pursuit. The boat rocked in an uneven, hypnotic rhythm from the gentle chop of the water. In another frame of mind, all would have been right with the world.

The pop of a soda can jerked Liz from her thoughts. Tyler handed her the cold can, smiled, and lifted his can in a toast. "Here's to nice girls who cry because of idiot guys."

"Sorry," said Liz. "I try not to cry in front of anyone. Mom always warned me about doing that."

He took a drink of soda and sat next to her. "Your mom is pretty tightly wound, isn't she?"

Liz chuckled. "You mean you noticed?" she said, her tone dripping with sarcasm.

"Such formality, stiffness, control. She actually fit in perfectly in Dad's house, in his world. As if she belonged in those museumlike rooms surrounded by finery and decorum."

"She does," Liz replied. She held the cold can to her forehead, relishing the chill cooling the feverish stir surging through her. "Mom is like one of those perfect porcelain dolls that's meant to live life in the comfort of a glass display case. Beautiful to look at but not meant to be touched. That was her existence when she was with the ballet. Adored by everyone from afar. But, so she said, she gave that up for marriage and for me."

"And I thought I was the only one to succumb to the old guilt trip," Tyler said, looking upward. He clinked his soda can on Liz's in a show of mock solidarity. "Here's to parents with crummy kids."

"What do you have to feel guilty about?" Liz looked into his eyes. "You're too old for high school antics." She couldn't hold back a smirk.

Tyler laughed. "Speeding across the football field, dumping red food coloring into the pool, and hiding the principal's car keys in the girls' bathroom were small potatoes compared to the things I feel guilty about now."

Liz's mouth opened. "*You* were the one who hid Mr. Schickling's keys?"

He flashed her a thumbs-up, and they both snickered at the memory.

"I'm just lucky that when the vice principal called to say my school ID had been found next to the keys, my father wasn't home, and my grandfather handled things. If it weren't for Gramp, I would have been dead meat." He exhaled and took a big slurp of soda.

"It's sweet, how close you were to your grandfather."

Tyler cast his eyes downward and kicked at the deck. He nodded. "That's what I feel guilty about."

"I don't understand." She sensed his vulnerability and held herself back from placing a hand on his arm.

"He would have liked you, Liz. A lot." Tyler turned toward her. "I can hear him say, 'Tyler, that fine girl deserves much more than to have you pretend to be her fiancé.'"

Liz cleared her throat and felt the flush in her cheeks heat up a few degrees.

"He would have been right, Liz. When you were at my father's house, and he was talking about us and our . . . wedding, it seemed so right. Like it was something, I don't know, something too special to be fake. It was wrong of me to ask you to pretend to be my fiancée, Liz. It was wrong of me to place you in this awkward situation. That's why I can't dance with you. It's not fair, and I don't want to hurt you."

Liz felt the darkening night air close in. He was right—something did seem terribly wrong. Where was the old, carefree, mischievous Tyler when she needed him? He'd picked a fine time to mature, to sprout feelings—to transform from the boy she remembered to the man she longed to know.

"Don't worry about me," she said. "We made a deal, an arrangement we can both benefit from. If anything's wrong, I'm just as much to blame as you are." Hesitating, she placed her hand on his. "The only way you can hurt me right now is to stop dancing."

Tyler stood, darkening the shadow in front of her. He took the soda can from Liz's hand and placed it on the deck. Then he pulled her to her feet and into his arms, looking at her with a longing that Liz found hard to interpret. "I'll count for us," he said. "If we're going to win that contest, we have to practice."

Liz took her stance and readied herself to dance. His posture had never looked quite so right, his form never quite so precise, his spirit never so determined. She had never wanted to dance more than she did at that moment.

"Ready?" Tyler asked. "Okay, then, one, two, three—"

"Together," she added quickly. And for the first time in their fortuitous pairing, and despite her best intentions, Liz knew she meant it for more than the dance.

Chapter Fourteen

"**M**aybe this isn't such a good idea." Liz sipped a seltzer as she and Tyler stood on the outskirts of the dance floor at the Olson Yacht Club. She tapped her foot to the jazzy tune played by the trio and glanced around to see who else was at the club.

"Sure it, is," said Tyler. "We need some real-life dance practice. The contest will be held in the United Veterans Association Hall, and that's a much bigger dance floor than your studio. We need to be ready for the real thing."

While Liz was overjoyed at Tyler's new commitment to win the contest, she was delightfully curious about his overzealous drive. Since their moonlight dance two nights before, he hadn't seemed to be able to get in enough practice. When he wasn't in the studio, he was calling her on the phone to discuss the dance moves, share his ideas, or inquire about the schedule for the next practice. He was like an athlete training for a marathon— focused and dedicated. As if he had way too much riding on this contest.

After the previous afternoon's three-hour practice, Liz was beat. When Tyler suggested they grab a hot dog at Joe's Lakeside Stand and then practice again, she had been pleasantly surprised. She was sure he must have been as tired as she was. Yet he'd wanted to persevere. She wasn't about to complain or discourage him— and she was afraid to question his newfound resolve. So she'd ordered a chocolate milkshake with her hot dog for extra energy, chastised herself about eating food that could cause her to gain weight and burst out of her dance costume, and then she and Tyler had danced until almost eleven at night.

Tyler really cared, and it raised an air of suspicion in Liz. Just as his insistence to go to the Yacht Club made her wonder if dancing was the only thing on his mind.

"Here comes a song with our fox-trot rhythm," said Tyler, as the trio broke into a bouncy version of "Pennies from Heaven." He pulled Liz to the center of the floor. "Let's do it."

"Good ear," she said as Tyler escorted her to the center of the dance floor, his hand held high, as if he were leading the queen.

"No, good teacher." He winked.

With little effort, they moved about the dance floor, their steps in perfect alignment, their moves a graceful show of competence and compatibility and proof positive of the fruits of practice and dedication. They looked as if they'd been dancing together for years. As if they were meant to move like one perfectly synchronized machine. The other dancers soon stepped aside, and when Liz finally broke her gaze from Tyler's gentle smile, she realized they were the only ones on the floor.

And she was thrilled.

When the song ended, the crowd clapped, Tyler embraced Liz, and they walked off the dance floor. If he weren't holding on to her, she would have floated away, soul weightless with joy.

"Let me tell you, Liz, you sure are something." Tyler delivered an affectionate squeeze. "Am I ever proud to dance with you."

All of those years of dance lessons, scrutiny under Grace's demanding and unappeasable eye, four years of dance college, dance internships every summer while her friends spent time lounging at the beach, watching her diet in an often futile attempt to keep her weight in check—all of it became worthwhile in that glorious second.

"Nice move for a sea dog," said an elderly, brawny man with a thick beard and scanty teeth who approached them.

"Thanks, Hal." Tyler shook the man's hand, eliciting an even wider toothless smile.

"Good to see you hold something other than a fishing rod in those hands," said the tall, angular-faced man with Hal.

"Hidden talents, Smitty," said Tyler with a self-deprecating tone. "Guys, this is my fiancée, Liz."

He didn't even stumble on the word, Liz noticed. She greeted the men.

"Mighty nice moves out there, miss," said Hal. "Or should I say *Mrs.?*" He let out a gravelly laugh.

Liz smiled at the men and then looked at Tyler, who continued to beam at her. Why was he so comfortable with this marriage masquerade? Apparently he was a good actor as well as a good dancer. She just hoped her acting would be so convincing when it came time for Tyler and her to part company—and she had to pretend she didn't care.

"I can see you've landed the catch of the day," Smitty said to Tyler. "Make sure you don't throw this one back in." He winked.

"I'll keep her on the line as long as I can," said Tyler, looking at Liz with a devilish glint in his eyes.

"That was great!" Tyler exclaimed, as he and Liz walked through the parking lot outside the yacht club. "We've got this dance contest in the bag for sure."

"There you go again, getting cocky. We can't afford to take anything for granted. Not with ten thousand dollars on the line." She hesitated and looked up at him with a bemused expression. "But, and don't let this go to your head, we were pretty impressive out there tonight."

"I knew even you, little Miss Doom and Gloom, couldn't deny it." His face lit up, and he wrapped his arms around her waist, picked her up, and twirled her in the air.

"Put me down, you idiot," Liz cried, though she was laughing as she said it. "Do you want to hurt yourself before the contest? We still have training to do."

"Hurt myself picking up a lithe thing like yourself? Hardly." All the same, he placed her on the ground. But he didn't remove his arms, which were still wrapped comfortably around her waist.

Liz could feel herself flush crimson. She wasn't sure if it was because of his compliment or the feel of his arms around her. She suspected it was a bit of both. She cast a cautious look upward at him. When she did, she saw that he was looking intently at her, his eyes sparkling. She knew what would happen if they kept staring at one another. She could feel it coming. Had felt it coming for weeks, if she was honest. And she knew she could end the moment with a word or a gesture. Instead, she held his gaze.

Tyler lowered his mouth to hers and kissed her gently. His lips were softer than she'd imagined they'd be, and she felt herself sink into the kiss, her lips responding to his just as her feet mirrored his on the dance floor. She could feel her heart pounding as the intensity of the kiss deepened. He traced his fingers down the side of her face and pulled her tighter against him. Her lips parted slightly, and her breath came in sharp, staccato pulses. As he ran his fingers through her hair, she felt as if she could stay like this forever.

Then, just as suddenly as it had begun, it was over. Tyler pulled away from her, dropped his arms to his sides, and stepped back. Had she done something wrong? she wondered. It had felt so right, so perfect. Kissing Tyler had turned out to be better, even, than dancing with him. So what had gone wrong? Something seemed to be bothering him.

"I'll bet it will be a huge relief for you when the dance contest is over," he said, not quite looking her in the eye.

"Well, yeah, I guess. It will be nice not to have to worry about money for a change." She wasn't quite sure what he was getting at, though she had a pretty good guess. "And then you won't have to pretend I'm your fiancée anymore."

"Right. Well, that will certainly make things easier."

Easier? She hadn't expected him to be quite that open about his relief. "Well, no need to worry about me. Once I've got the money from the dance contest and my mom is back on solid ground, I'll be back in Syracuse and out of your hair." It pained her to even say the words, but it seemed like what he wanted to hear. It wasn't long ago that she had longed to get back to Syracuse. But that was before Tyler. Before everything. Now Syracuse was the last place she wanted to be.

"Yeah. I'm sure my dad won't be so pleased about the broken engagement, but he'll get over it once I pay back the trust."

So it really was all about the money to him. How

could she have been so naïve? She'd really thought that Tyler had changed. But this was the same old love-'em-and-leave-'em Tyler Augustine she remembered from high school. The kiss hadn't meant anything to him. He'd gotten caught up in the moment and now was trying to distance himself. After all, she was only his fake fiancée. He wouldn't want an accidental fling clouding the issue.

He glanced at his watch. "Wow, it's getting kind of late. I should get you home if we're going to practice bright and early tomorrow."

She was mortified. And more than that, she was angry. Angry at him for being so selfish and angry at herself for thinking it could be different, that he'd changed. That he'd changed for her.

He walked her to the car and politely opened the door for her but wouldn't look her in the eye. Liz sat quietly in the passenger seat, not saying a word the entire ride home. She was afraid what might happen if she did. Either she'd scream at him, or she'd burst into tears. Neither was a particularly appealing option. When Tyler pulled up in front of her house, she reached quickly for the door handle.

"So, I guess I'll see you in the morning," she said with as much false cheer as she could muster. If he wanted to pretend nothing had happened, well, two could play at that game.

"Yup. Sure will." He turned toward her, and she saw

that the smile he had plastered onto his face didn't quite reach his eyes.

"Idiot!" Tyler yelled at himself while he pounded a fist on the steering wheel.

That was maybe the stupidest thing he'd ever done. How could he kiss her like that? The truth was, he could have gone on kissing her all night. But he'd had to stop. He wasn't good enough for Liz Pruitt—never had been, never would be. He knew it, and he knew that, deep down, whether she admitted it or not, she knew it. But he'd gotten caught up in the moment. When she'd looked up at him through those dark lashes, he couldn't help himself.

But he should have. This was a purely professional relationship. Liz had made that clear from the start. She was a serious-minded girl, and this dance contest meant her livelihood and that of her mother. He'd thought maybe he'd begun to sense a sort of change in her, a softening, as if maybe she was warming to him. She'd started to loosen up and have more fun, like at the yacht club earlier that evening.

And then when he'd kissed her, she'd kissed him back. Hadn't she? He couldn't be sure. But when he'd asked her about the dance contest, she'd mentioned the money and the dance studio, and he knew that she was still focused on the contest. Not on him.

So they'd stick to the plan. They'd both get their

money and then part ways. As they had planned it. As it should be. They'd both have everything they wanted.

So why did it feel as if he'd just had everything taken away?

"I didn't expect you home so early," said Grace, crutches and cast thudding into the living room where Liz sat staring at the blank television screen.

"It's eleven, not that early," Liz replied.

Grace lowered herself into the chair across from Liz and placed her crutches on the floor. "Eleven is early for a date to end."

"I wasn't on a date, Mom," said Liz emphatically. "Tyler and I were just practicing our routine outside the studio."

Grace stretched her lips into that perfect, boxy shape that the trained eye could have interpreted as a sophisticated smile meant to limit creasing around the mouth. She folded her hands in her lap.

An uneasy silence accompanied by the familiar chill Grace often elicited filled the room.

"You think Tyler and I were on a date?" Liz snapped.

"I didn't say that," Grace replied calmly.

"But you thought it," Liz retorted, curling her legs under herself and adjusting the pillow behind her back.

"So now my daughter reads my mind."

Liz didn't respond. She rubbed her temples as the familiar tension surfaced.

Grace spoke quietly. "And what am I thinking now?"

Liz faced her mother. The spunk in her attitude quickly dissipated when she saw an uncharacteristic warmth in Grace's eyes. "You're thinking I'm a fool to have fallen in love with Tyler Augustine."

"No, but I do think you're a fool to deny your feelings."

Liz moved to the edge of the couch, inching closer to her mother. "You do? Really?"

Grace nodded. "Have you any idea how rare true love is? Don't spend your life wanting."

Liz was taken aback by the profundity and mystery in her mother's statement. Had Grace spent her whole life wanting? Had Liz confused her loneliness with her stoic manner? "I . . . I think the dancing made me love him."

"Or did loving him give you a renewed passion for dancing? I know how easily love and dance can become intertwined." Grace closed her eyes, and her face softened, as if she was savoring some delightful memories.

"What should I do, Mom?" asked Liz. "Listen to my heart?"

Grace opened her eyes and reached out, her fingertips just grazing her daughter's cheek. "Yes, and also listen to your feet."

Liz looked down at her naked size tens, callused from years of dancing, toes twisted from being shoved into countless pairs of heels, indentations from T straps that had cinched her like a vise. If her feet could talk, they'd beg for a pedicure and a hot epsom salt soak. Her feet were too smart to tell her to fall for a fisherman who was destined to become the one who got away as soon as this dance contest was over. He'd made that clear.

But her heart . . . well, that was another story.

Tyler noticed light shining from under the door of Agnes' suite. He stood outside the door, raised a fist, hesitated, and then knocked with three quick taps, entering when she answered.

"Honey, what is it?" asked Agnes, her face taking on a look that anticipated disaster. Dressed in a green chenille bathrobe and quilted slippers, she sat in an overstuffed recliner by the window, an open book in her lap. A few curlers surrounded her face like a halo of pink plastic sausages. "Thought you went out with Liz."

"We were at the dance at the yacht club, but we left when the band took a break. Liz said she was tired."

"And was she?"

Tyler looked down and rotated his ankle, noting the pleasant, exercised feeling of his lower leg. The dancing was challenging him in ways he'd never even considered. And it felt good. "Who knows?" He raised his eyes to Agnes. "Maybe she's just tired of me."

"You've probably worn down the poor girl with all that dancing." Agnes placed a bookmark between the pages and gently closed the cover. "Come over here and talk to me."

Tyler sat cross-legged on the floor in front of Agnes' chair, one of his favorite places in the house. As a child, he'd sat in that same spot almost every evening while Agnes read to him. It was the best time of his day. The house was dark and warm, the aroma of the delicious dinner they'd just eaten lingered, and he had the undivided attention of the woman who made a valiant effort to be a substitute mother to a spoiled kid who would never realize how lucky he was. When Agnes read, Tyler loved the animation in her voice, the crazy faces she made to accompany the story, the hand gestures that formed monstrous patterns on the wall. And when the story ended, Tyler was guaranteed a bear hug that caused him to melt into Agnes' soft, fleshy embrace.

"So I agreed to dance with Liz to make a few bucks," he began, not waiting for Agnes to inquire further. "I did *not* intend to fall in love with her. No way, no how."

"Maybe you're just infatuated with the chance to spend some time with a pretty girl," Agnes added. "Been quite awhile since I heard you even mention a girlfriend's name."

Tyler smiled sheepishly. "Well, as Dad will happily tell you, a guy like me who prefers to wander around and spend his time on a boat isn't exactly every lady's idea of the ideal guy for a long-term relationship."

Agnes pointed at him and kicked off her slippers. "Despite what your father says, don't you believe for one second that you're not a good catch for some lucky girl. Don't try to make me believe you didn't have fun with those girls you dated. It was the right thing at the time."

Tyler traced the curvy pattern in the rug with one finger. "Okay, so I had fun. But it was so fleeting. Sure, they were nice girls, but . . ."

"But they weren't Liz," Agnes chimed in quickly through pursed lips. "They weren't sweet, pretty, smart, talented, and kind, all rolled into one."

He shifted his legs and bent forward. "That she is," said Tyler, his voice drifting. "She also is way more concerned with dancing than she'll ever be with me. Once this contest is over, Liz Pruitt will be out of my life. She's made that perfectly clear."

"So what do you plan to do about that?" asked Agnes pointedly, hands poised in a steeple under her chin.

Tyler shrugged. "Not much I can do."

"Come on, honey. Get that brain working." Agnes clapped her hands to draw his attention.

Tyler plopped flat on the floor, arms outstretched at his sides.

Agnes nudged his leg with her bare foot. "Come on now." She inhaled deeply before speaking. "Don't start acting like the caricature your father created."

Tyler bolted upright, a little fire smoldering inside as the truth in Agnes' words hit home. No, the last thing he'd be was the person his father thought he was. Tyler Augustine would not be the carefree drifter who let life pass him by—let Liz pass him by—while he spent the day moored on a boat that didn't run, hoping for things to be different. Waiting for the next dance. "If Liz knows

I care enough about her to throw my whole self into this contest, maybe I'll have a chance."

Agnes gave him a thumbs-up.

"Time for my feet and heart to start communicating," Tyler replied.

Chapter Fifteen

"So we're having an off day." Tyler flung a rolled white towel around his neck to absorb his perspiration and paced to the window. Damp tendrils of blond hair stuck to his temples. He leaned on the sill of the open window so the outside air could cool his skin.

Liz shuddered and combed her fingers through her hair, wading through the tangled curls. "But we can't afford to have an off day," she moaned. "The contest is just three days away. Three days! We should be at our best now, not floundering." She put her hands over her face and shook in frustration. "What is going on with us?"

Tyler sauntered back to Liz and placed an arm around her shoulders. "Liz, you know we can do this. Let's just keep cool."

Liz shook off his arm with a flick of her shoulder.

"We used to be able to do this, but now we can't. I don't get it." She raised her hands in disbelief. "We know the steps. We know the song. We're doing the right moves. But we're not dancing."

Tyler took her hands in his and looked straight into her eyes, commanding her attention. "Let's try again."

Liz took a deep breath, nodded, and motioned for him to turn on the music. She prepared to concentrate, center her attention on the moment, on the dance. When the sprightly tune filled the room, they took their positions, face-to-face, waiting for their cue. Tyler was serious. Not even a hint of his usual wisecracking smile. Liz knew he wanted this dance to work out as much as she did.

Like a matador's anticipating the charge of a bull, Liz's heart pounded as she waited for the correct down-beat. Tyler watched her with intensity, waiting for that almost imperceptible lift of her eyebrow that signaled them to take the first step.

At the exact moment, they started their fox-trot around the perimeter of the studio. The first set of steps was on beat and executed to perfection. On the second repeat of that same set, they fumbled on a simple turn meant to twist Liz backward, drop her quickly into Tyler's arms, and then spin her upright and out again.

They stopped, and Liz pounded the air with knotted fists. "Ugh! We've done that flawlessly a million times. Maybe more. What just happened?"

"I must have done something wrong," said Tyler, lowering his head and shaking it.

"It's not you." Liz wished she could inject a more compassionate tone into her voice, let him know she was touched at his willingness to take the blame for something he hadn't done. Tyler had been doing all of his steps exactly as Liz had taught him. He rarely missed a beat, and he added more flair to the dance than she ever could have hoped. No, this wasn't his fault.

Yet it wasn't hers either.

She had to give herself some credit. Not an easy thing for her to do. Her dancing was on its game. She'd done this routine countless times. She'd taught it to legions of people. Her dance professor in college had even had her demonstrate her finesse to the class. No, Liz was doing everything right. Just as Tyler was.

They just weren't doing it right . . . together.

Liz had no answer. But she knew someone who would.

"Wait right here," she said to Tyler, sprinting through the door that led to the house.

Liz found Grace sitting by the living room window, reading her poetry and listening to classical music. She stood in front of her mother, saying nothing, waiting for Grace to give her permission to speak, as she'd been taught to do as a child.

When Grace finished the poem, she acknowledged her daughter by looking upward and arching her eyebrows.

"We need your help with our routine," Liz said quickly, forcing out the words before she could change her mind.

Grace gestured to her casted leg. "As you can see, my dancing has been halted, perhaps for eternity. There's no telling what atrophy has consumed my leg and destroyed my life. I can't help you dance, Liz. Not now, maybe not ever."

Liz knelt and placed a hand on her mother's arm. "Now's not the time for drama, Mom. I don't need you to dance. I need you to coach us. Watch us. Something is wrong, and I don't know what it is."

Grace closed her book and placed her crossed hands on the cover. "And what makes you think I'll know?"

Liz stood, towering over Grace. "You taught me how to dance. Anyone who can make a dancer out of *this* must know how to work miracles." She gestured with a sweep from head to toe.

Grace furrowed her brow. "Enough with the flattery, Liz. You're strong, tall, muscular, and beautiful. You were born a dancer, my dear. My lessons just put a high shine on that gold, polishing it into the precious metal it was destined to be. Don't give me credit for who you are."

Liz was speechless. Her mouth gaped open as she grappled for something to say and came up empty. Had her mother really just complimented her? Had she really delivered not just a few kind words but an Academy Award-sized presentation of affection? Maybe the same weird energy that was preventing her and Tyler from dancing had altered her mother's mind.

Grace reached for her crutches and stood. "Let's get to work."

When the song ended, Liz finally allowed herself to breathe, even though she didn't dare move. She and Tyler stood before Grace, frozen in the final step of the dance—arms around each other, shoulders straight, chin high—awaiting the verdict.

Grace stood silently, leaning on her crutches, still scrutinizing them even though the dance had ended. Her green eyes zipped wildly up and down their bodies. She tilted her head and looked at them from all possible angles. "How did it feel?" she asked, her gaze focused on Liz.

"No missteps," Liz commented. "We stayed with the beat."

"How did it feel?" Grace asked again.

"I thought we coordinated the spin ending the first verse really well. We didn't trip, and our upper bodies remained relaxed but attentive."

Grace ungripped the crutches and struck her hands together, creating one sharp beat that resounded in the studio. "Listen to what I'm asking you, Elizabeth. How did it *feel?*"

Liz released her arms from Tyler, vulnerable as the rigid but comforting tension of his grip left her to stand alone. "It felt like nothing," she responded quietly, flatly. "Nothing."

"Flawless execution isn't dance," said Grace, reveling

in her milieu. "*This* is dance," she said, pointing to her heart. "Your feet are doing exactly what they're supposed to do, but don't confuse knowing a routine with dancing. Now, work on the heart—and then you'll be dancing." She turned and shuffled back into the house, each thump of her crutches stabbing at Liz with painful truth.

"Well, one thing is certain—you'll be the prettiest couple in the contest," said Agnes, her lips tightly clenching straight pins as she positioned herself in front of the wooden stool on which Tyler stood. She motioned for him to straighten his arms as she pinned the hems of his sleeves.

"I'll never be able to dance in this tux." Tyler caught a glimpse of himself in the studio mirrors. He flexed his shoulders and grimaced at the restriction of the jacket. "With any luck, we'll look so good, they won't notice the dancing."

"Shh," Agnes hissed. "The girls are just over there in the dressing room. Don't let Liz hear you. You'll hurt her feelings. Stand straight."

Tyler stiffened his posture as Agnes gently lowered herself to a kneeling position, groaned as her formidable body settled on the floor, and pulled on the bottom of Tyler's trousers. She carefully marked the hems with a piece of chalk and placed pins where a stitch was required.

"No wiggling," demanded Agnes. "So what's this doubt about not being able to win the contest?"

Tyler looked down at Agnes' gray curls. "We started out with a bang, but lately we've been stinking up the joint."

"Still a couple of days to practice." Agnes placed the last pin from her mouth into the hem and reached for another on the tomato-shaped pincushion fastened around her left wrist. "Not like you to give up, honey."

"Ouch," said Tyler when Agnes stuck his ankle with a pin.

"Sorry. Now stop slouching, unless you want a few more pinpricks to the leg."

"Liz even had to ask her mother for pointers."

Agnes started to heft herself upward, and Tyler reached down and helped yank her to her feet. She rubbed the small of her back and then smoothed Tyler's jacket, studying his reflection in the mirror. "Too loose?" She cinched the back of the jacket to tighten it around his middle. "Show off that slim waist, and get some payback for all those hours you spend at the gym."

"Fits well," Tyler responded. "Last thing I need is to feel like I'm in a straitjacket. I'd rather be wearing my fishing vest."

"So, did Grace give any helpful advice?" Agnes reached to inspect the back of the collar.

"She said we know the steps, but we don't have any feeling." He shrugged.

"Turn toward me." Tyler turned, and Agnes studied the lapels, smoothing them at the seams. She folded a red silk handkerchief and placed it in the breast pocket. "Do you?"

"What?" asked Tyler, silently approving of his reflection in the mirror. He hadn't worn a tuxedo since his senior prom. And that was one night he hoped to wipe from his memory bank. At the time he'd thought asking Rose Garrie, the head cheerleader and class flirt, was the right thing to do. When she left with the exchange student from England before the prom was over, Tyler had spent the rest of the evening sitting on the steps outside the school so he wouldn't have to explain to his friends that he'd been dumped for a poor man's Paul McCartney. He could only hope that this tuxedo-wearing event wouldn't be accompanied by similar disaster.

"Do you have any feeling when you dance with Liz?" Agnes stood back and nodded approvingly at her handiwork.

Any feeling? He had *every* feeling. Pride at how well they danced together. Joy to have Liz in his arms. Amusement to see the twinkle in her eye when the move was right and the frown when they could have done better. Regret to think what a fool he'd been to ignore her all those years ago.

Fear—to know that when the contest ended, so would they.

"Red is your color." Julie fastened the satin-covered buttons on the back of Liz's dress.

Liz turned on the wooden stool to catch a full view of herself in the cheval mirror located in a corner of the studio's dressing room. If modesty hadn't been one of the virtues Grace had pounded into her, she would have found the courage to compliment the woman in the mirror. She looked more chic and sparkling than she could have imagined. Too bad her dour expression ruined the elegance of the dress.

The red satin, floor-length gown shimmered even in the dim light of the dressing room. A full chiffon skirt ruffled outward from the waist, presenting a dramatic accent to the scoop-necked, rhinestone-studded bodice. Chiffon sleeves hung loosely to the wrist, making her arms appear as if they were floating in clouds of scarlet. She remembered her mother's saying that a timid dancer always played it safe and wore black; a true professional was brave and wore red. Was it too late to change colors?

"You don't think it's too bold?" Liz studied her profile in the mirror.

"Bold? Get with it, Liz. You're in a dance contest, not entering a convent. If you can't be bold now, when will you ever have the chance to be?" Julie pinned a red sash accented with silver threads tightly around Liz's waist, accentuating her hourglass figure.

Julie was right. Liz had just this one chance to risk it all. One chance. Just a few minutes on the dance floor would decide her fate. As soon as she took that first step, turning back would no longer be an option. She'd walk away victorious and ten thousand dollars richer, or she'd walk away broke—and alone. Her soul poorer than her empty pockets.

"What jewelry do you think I should wear?" asked Liz.

"Just the rock." Julie held up Liz's left hand. "This is so magnificent that no other jewelry deserves to be within a mile's radius of it. It was a good idea to wear it for the costume fitting so we could see how it looks with the dress. Did you ever see anything like it? I can't take my eyes off it. Shame it's just a loaner."

Julie had apparently not noticed that Liz had been wearing the ring for days. She'd have to relinquish it soon enough after the contest. Something about the hunk of refined carbon and platinum gave her hope. She liked looking at her hand and fantasizing, just for a while, about how delightful it was to be the future Mrs. Tyler Augustine—even the fake version.

"Getting nervous?" Julie pinned the slight gap in the low back of the dress. "Do you think this needs to be taken in a touch so it stays nice and tight when you bend backward?"

"Yes, uh, no," Liz stammered.

"Huh?"

"Yes on the dress; no on the nerves." She glanced at the diamond on her hand, looking for a little strength.

"I'd think even a pro like you would get butterflies before a performance. Especially with Adonis as your partner." Julie stretched her neck so Liz could see her in the reflection of the mirror and winked saucily.

"Just enough butterflies to keep it interesting." Liz didn't want to tell Julie that she wasn't terrified to dance, but she was plenty scared about what would happen when the contest ended. Panic-stricken about the moment she'd have to take the ring from her finger and place it back in Tyler's hand.

That moment when the ring returned to being the prop it was intended to be instead of the symbol of hope it had become.

Julie skipped into the studio, clapping her hands excitedly. "Get ready, you two," she called loudly. "Let's try out your costumes so Agnes and I can see. Pretend this is the contest." She trilled a drumroll off her tongue as she turned on the stereo.

Liz breathed deeply, mustering up the inner strength she had always counted on but that now seemed to fight desperately to elude her. She glanced quickly at herself in the mirror; at least she looked the part. She shuffled the opening steps; she definitely knew the steps. She looked at the engagement ring on her left hand. . . .

And searched for the feeling Grace had spoken of.

When the introductory measures of "It's De-Lovely" permeated the studio, she glided onto the highly polished wooden floor, her shoes reflecting in the brilliant shine. Then she let the music transport her to that place where her feelings were supposed to reside, where she hoped to find them.

And then she saw Tyler.

Liz fought the emotion that swelled in her throat when he approached her on the dance floor. She could have overlooked the fact that he was the most handsome man she had ever seen. She could have closed her eyes and feasted forever on the vision that was branded into her mind. And she could have been buried alive by a Lake Ontario lake-effect snowstorm and still burned up with the heat that surrounded her.

But she couldn't deny the feeling that burst from each cell in her body, promising to propel her across the dance floor like the effortless flutter of a butterfly. The feeling that she had danced with Tyler infinite times before yet was about to experience it for the first time.

As Liz and Tyler locked arms and prepared to dance, she glanced over his shoulder and saw Grace standing in the doorway. Grace pointed to her heart. And she offered Liz a smile that was wider than any Liz had seen from her mother in her twenty-nine years.

And then the dance began. The music carried Liz and Tyler across the floor, not two people but one couple. Her feet were moving, but she never felt the floor. Tyler was inches from her, yet she couldn't distinguish his soul from hers.

Their feet moved in unison, one step leading to the next with fluidity and panache. Arms clasped, released, and clasped again, just as they needed to. When Liz separated from Tyler for those quick moments, she returned to him eagerly, his energy calling her back.

They smiled naturally, and when the routine called

for their eyes to part, Liz easily found her spot again in the eager longing on Tyler's face. As if he was living for that moment when she was once again locked safely in his view.

Liz heard the music, yet the sounds were a million miles away, drowned out by the beat of her heart. Julie, Agnes, and Grace were watching them, their faces frozen like those of smiling mannequins, yet there was no one in the room but Tyler.

Just Tyler.

And then the dance ended.

"Thank goodness the costumes didn't fall apart," said Agnes.

Liz and Tyler remained locked in the final step of their dance, eyes riveted on each other, unable to part. "Yes, thank goodness," Liz said distantly.

"Yeah," Tyler added, his voice drifting but his eyes fixed on Liz.

"*Nothing* fell apart," commented Julie, her eyes misting when Liz glanced her way.

Liz looked over Tyler's shoulder at her mother. Grace brushed a tear from her cheek and placed a hand on her heart. She positioned the crutches under her arms, turned, and walked back into the house.

"A performance of that caliber deserves a celebration." Julie hurried to the desk to uncover some containers of food she'd brought over earlier.

"I knew I smelled peach cobbler," said Agnes,

making a beeline for the desk. "Watching all that danc-ing made me work up an appetite."

"Hungry?" Tyler asked Liz, still in his embrace as if the song hadn't ended. Never would.

She shook her head, her throat feeling tight.

"Perfect, right?" he asked.

If the dance was the only thing on her mind, Liz would have readily agreed. Yes, the dance was perfect. They didn't miss a step. They looked as if they'd been born in each other's arms, meant to dance together always. Like they belonged together. Like they were one.

"I need some air." Liz broke free from Tyler's em-brace and hurried out the door.

Chapter Sixteen

"Have some cake, honey," said Agnes, handing Tyler a plate of dark-chocolate cake iced with white icing swirled into stiff peaks and dusted with grated coconut. "Julie baked her little heart out on this one."

Tyler accepted the plate, scooped up a forkful, and then placed the fork back on the plate without eating the cake.

"I've never known you to pass up good food," Agnes replied. "What's up?"

"I'm worried about Liz. She's been so gung ho on winning this contest. We finally had a breakthrough performance, and she disappears. That's not like her." He loosened his tie and wrinkled his brow.

"She's only been gone for twenty minutes. She'll be back."

Tyler placed a hand on Agnes' shoulder. "Why did she leave? I thought everything felt great."

Agnes grinned and lowered her voice in a maternal whisper. "That's why she left, honey."

He shrugged. "You've lost me. Liz said we needed to have all this feeling."

Tyler's soul dipped. Oh, he had feelings all right. When he saw Liz on that dance floor, draped in red, glowing like a garnet, he was sure any dance moves he'd learned would be erased from his brain. He was dumbfounded. She was the most beautiful woman he'd ever seen. Poised, strong, elegant—Liz Pruitt was way more woman than he deserved to have. He cursed those years in high school when he'd been so caught up in his own bravado that he'd failed to form a friendship with her. And then he'd let almost a dozen more years pass while he drifted around the world, looking for something, someone, he could have found in his own backyard.

When Tyler took Liz into his arms and they started dancing, he'd almost suffocated—happily—in her aura. The intense energy from her touch, the electricity of being just inches from her angelic face. If those were the feelings Liz had said they needed, then he'd reaped more than his fair share. And if those feelings weren't enough, he'd never be able to do better. Never be able to . . . to love her more.

"You showed her all those feelings. And now she has to deal with it," Agnes added.

Tyler set the cake plate on the desk, licking his

thumb where he'd touched some frosting. "So she left because she got what she wanted and now she doesn't know what to do?"

Agnes picked up Tyler's plate and ate a forkful of cake. "Now you're picking up the drift." She licked her lips. "This cake is to die for."

He put his hands into his tuxedo jacket's pockets and paced to the window and then back to Agnes. "I don't know what secret psychology takes place inside you ladies, and I can't even begin to figure it out. But one thing I do know—this explains why I'm almost thirty and had to bribe a girl to pretend to be my fiancée. Know what, Agnes? Maybe I don't deserve a good woman like Liz."

Agnes put down the plate with a bang. "Don't you ever think that," she said emphatically. "You're one of the most genuine, kind souls I've ever met. You're the man every woman longs to be with and the one she thinks she'll never be lucky enough to have. And then luck surprises her—so she runs."

Tyler thought for a second, grabbed his motorcycle keys from the desk, and ran out the door.

So Liz felt it too.

"I hate to be the one to break it to you, but the prom was about twelve years ago," said Tyler to Liz, motioning to her dress as he approached her huddled on the bottom step of the bleachers in the high school stadium. He sat next to her.

"I know," she replied. "Julie and I played three games of Monopoly and ate an entire pan of brownies that night."

Tyler looked around the stadium, the metal bleachers catching the moonbeams as the clouds drifted silently throughout the sky, giving way to a scattering of stars that showed their brilliance and then retreated shyly beneath the clouds, waiting for just the right stargazer to twinkle for. "Boy, this place looks a lot smaller than I remember."

"How about the time you threw the winning touchdown pass, and the Olson Buccaneers won the division championship right in this spot?" Liz twisted the red satin sash on her dress.

Tyler grinned. "I forgot about that. Pretty cool, huh? You were there?"

She shook her head. "I was at a dance competition in Manhattan. Julie told me about it."

"And you won a trophy, right?" Tyler elbowed her and winked.

"Yes, but . . . How did you find me, anyway?" She sat up straight and placed her hands on her hips, glaring at him, while a light breeze picked up and blew a lock of hair into her eyes.

"I thought I'd go back to the place where it all started. Where I first met an incredibly cute, shy girl who never let a mouthful of braces stop her from smiling and who was always kind to the spoiled rich kid who was way too big for his britches." He reached for her hand.

"That's really . . . romantic," she said, lowering her eyes.

Tyler puffed out a breath. "Okay, big confession. I also stopped at Josh's gas station on the corner to ask if anyone saw you. Josh saw a woman in a long dress walk by a little while ago. At this end of town there are only two choices: the school or the dump. I can't see you going to a dump in that dress."

Liz couldn't hold back her smile. "I like an honest guy." She squeezed his hand tighter.

"And I like an honest girl," Tyler added. "So how about 'fessing up and telling me why you left?"

Liz exhaled and looked up at the moon. For a moment the clouds had parted for a bright, three-quarter moon. Only a hint of how magnificent it was going to be when it was full, ready, finished. She glanced at the diamond ring. "You felt it too. Didn't you? While we were dancing."

"That was the idea, right?"

Liz turned to look at Tyler, locking on to his gaze. She had to make him understand he'd done nothing wrong. "Tyler, I felt things that were too special, too wonderful, to be subjected to false engagements, empty bank accounts, domineering mothers, insistent fathers . . . ghosts from the past. I needed to get out of that studio and leave those feelings behind." A bubble of tears covered her eyes.

"Did you? Leave them behind?"

She shook her head slowly and grasped his hand

tighter while the tears trickled down her cheeks. "What should we do?" she said in almost a whisper.

Tyler stood and pulled her to her feet. "Well, here we are back at high school. And we both sure look like we're dressed for the prom." He hesitated. "Shall we dance?"

Tyler pulled Liz to the middle of the stadium, moonlight leading the way. He positioned his arms around her. "Ready? One, two, three . . . together," he said, as they glided around the stadium, guided by the music in their hearts, eyes locked on each other, feet moving to the rhythm in their souls.

"Yes, together," Liz repeated quietly.

Chapter Seventeen

"**L**et's hear it, folks, for our first couple tonight: Miss Shelly Hennessey and Mr. Mike Clark," bellowed the announcer as the music kicked in, the dance floor dimmed, and the audience cheered.

Liz took a deep breath. The ballroom dance contest. The moment she'd been waiting for, training for, hoping for. Weeks of preparation, soul-searching, bliss, and heartache had led to this moment. Her emotions were playing a high-stakes game of tug-of-war, joyful for the night yet dreading its end.

The United Veterans Association Hall, Olson's largest social club, had been transformed into a theatrical wonderland by the contest sponsors. Rows of folding chairs surrounded the dance floor, sandwiching in over five hundred people but still unable to accommodate other eager onlookers who lined the sides of the room. This contest was big news for Olson, for upstate New York. Bigger news for Liz.

Sparkling disco balls hung from the ceilings, splashing prismatic twinkles across the dance floor. The ten-piece Jimmy Jazz Orchestra, complete with wooden music stands emblazoned with the letters *JJ,* perched atop a raised platform and was awash in a flood of lights. The musicians' glittering blue jackets with satin lapels shone in the glow of the metal instruments. The tuxedo-clad announcer held a microphone and stood next to the orchestra to announce each couple, cajole the audience to be active participants, and shamelessly publicize the contest sponsors.

Watching through the window in a large wooden door from the adjoining room, Liz located her mother, Julie, Agnes, and Sam. As she feared, they sat in the front row, directly in line with forward-moving steps that dominated the dance she and Tyler would perform. Just great. They would be right in the line of fire. Grace would scrutinize them with a merciless gaze, her sharp green eyes boring through them with laserlike intensity. No, Grace wouldn't miss a step. And there would be no way that Liz could miss Grace.

Sam looked uncomfortable. He rotated his head, looking around the room, seemingly to find out if anyone in the audience recognized him. Tyler had said earlier that he wasn't sure if Sam would attend the contest, citing it as an undignified activity and yet another way Tyler had found to waste his time. His only positive comment was that at least they were doing ballroom dance and not hip-hop.

When Liz mentioned to Tyler that his father was in the audience, Tyler shrugged as if he didn't care; but then he smiled when he thought she wasn't looking. Liz was glad Sam had decided to attend, and she was curious what his reaction would be to his son's mastery of the fox-trot.

Liz studied the first couple as they took their place and began to dance. She watched the judges observe the dancers, jot notes, and look over glasses slid down on their noses while the audience reacted. She was so intent on the logistics taking place in and around the dance floor that she barely noticed Tyler approach her from behind.

"I don't understand why you're gawking at the competition," he said with a tsk-tsk. "You're just getting yourself worked up over nothing."

She motioned with a hand for him to keep his voice down. "Knowing the competition is the lifeblood of performance dance," Liz whispered, her eyes riveted on the couple. She moved her feet, mimicking the couple's moves. "Sometimes being good isn't enough. But being better than everyone else is always important."

"We can do whatever they do, only better," said Tyler, the hesitation in his voice telling Liz he wasn't as confident as he tried to sound. He walked away from Liz and sat, resting his head in his hands.

"She looks as if she's floating on a cloud," said Liz, eyes still locked on the dancers. "Very nice moves. Great posture."

"Uh-huh," Tyler commented.

As Liz watched the next two couples dance, her tension mounted. Some nervousness was healthy before a show. Required, almost. Nervous anticipation had often proven to be her best friend, forcing her to exceed her personal best many times. She'd seen a healthy dose of the jitters transform Grace into a magnificent vision on stage when the jolts of tension surged through her, driving her to that one glorious moment when she owned the world. When she was the star. Now it was Liz's turn to be the star—and share the sky with Tyler.

"Think they're better than us?" Tyler stood from the chair, paced to the back of the room, then walked to Liz, peeking through the window over her shoulder.

"Doesn't matter what I think," she replied, her lips moving as she silently counted their steps. "But they sure have a flair that would make any judge take notice."

"I hadn't noticed." Tyler watched silently for a few more seconds. "See my father? He actually looks as if he's enjoying himself."

Liz followed Tyler's gaze to Sam's smiling face. "He does look happy. Just wait until he sees his boy dance." She shot Tyler a broad smile, thinking of how proud Sam would be.

He took one last glance at his father before moving away from the door.

"Get ready. We're next." Liz inhaled deeply and smoothed her skirt, straightened her neckline, and tightened the sash. She adjusted Tyler's bow tie and fluffed the silk hanky in his pocket. She reached to flatten a curl on the neckline she'd come to know so well, then lowered her hand. No, this was one area she wouldn't tamper with. It was perfect in its very special way.

Tyler smirked. "So, how do we look?"

"Too cute for our own good," Liz replied sarcastically. "But if we don't deliver, all the 'cute' in the universe won't cut it."

"It's going to be tough for me to concentrate on my dance steps with a beauty like you in my arms." He winked and took her hand, fingering the diamond deliberately.

Tyler's words were pushed aside by the panic that ripped through Liz as she listened to the current dancers' song wind down. Never had so much ridden on one competition. She'd vied for trophies, acceptance to dance academies, final grades in her classes, even her mother's approval. All of those spoils paled in comparison to the prize offered by tonight's competition.

And the ten thousand dollars wasn't even on her mind.

"Tyler," she said softly, "do you really . . . really care about winning? About . . . us winning?"

Tyler cocked his head, expression softening. He inched closer. "What more can I say to convince you how much I care? What do I have to do, Liz? Tell you . . . tell you that I love you?"

Liz's mouth dropped open, and she felt herself freeze. She was speechless, barely breathing. Stunned. Had she heard Tyler correctly? *Love?* Did he mean those fateful words? Surely he was just making an off-the-cuff statement, talking in general terms.

"What?" Liz eked out through a throat tight with emotion before she heard the announcer introduce them.

Tyler gave her a quick peck on the cheek, grabbed her hand, and led her out the door as the orchestra struck up the opening bars of "It's De-Lovely." It was showtime. They sprinted gracefully to the center of the dance floor, megawatt smiles plastered on their faces, and posed for the opening step.

They waited with joyful anticipation for the music and their feet to link up, turn them into winners. Liz tried to center herself, concentrate on every detail as she mentally prepared for what might be one of the most important events of her life.

Her senses were on high alert. Tyler's hands on her back felt warmer than she remembered. She attributed that to the hot overhead lights. His eyes had a sparkle she didn't recall seeing before. But whose eyes wouldn't shine so marvelously under the disco balls? Had he always been this tall, this well proportioned? A perfect fit as she gripped him for dear life, melding herself into him. How could something they'd done numerous times before carry with it the anxiety of a maiden voyage?

Then the dance began. First one step, then another, then another, until their motion was a chain reaction of wildly moving feet, zigzagging in and out of each other's, stepping with a delicate pattern delivered with the force and verve of deliberate strength. Liz and Tyler were in perfect harmony. Their weight shifted on cue, and Tyler felt like an extension of Liz's own body. When the dance separated them for a second, they remained connected by an invisible energy that returned them to each other as if being together was their destiny. Each turn, dip, and bend was executed with expert precision.

Liz felt Tyler's hand brush across her back, down her arm, and around her shoulders with an electricity that could have illuminated the darkest night. When their faces neared, she felt his breathing, timed exactly with hers. They weren't just dancing; they had become one entity, one spirit. As if moved by an ethereal force, they commanded the dance floor. Claimed each other's souls.

Yes, this was the way to dance.

When the song ended, Tyler and Liz held their final pose in the middle of the dance floor. His arm was around her waist as she turned to the side, hands arched in a relaxed pyramid at her chest, head lifted high, a rehearsed, coquettish upturn of her lips. She counted to ten, and then she and Tyler broke their pose amid thundering applause, whistles, and hoots.

Liz looked toward her mother. Grace remained seated. She didn't clap, didn't smile. But tears poured down her cheeks, so all Liz could see in the darkened hall were great emerald eyes, twinkling with tears.

Grace raised a hand to her heart and patted her chest. Then she placed both her hands on her lips and threw Liz a kiss with gentle vehemence. Liz felt lighter than a feather, released of a burden that had weighed her down her whole life. Her soul was lifted, her spirit steeped with life. Her mother was overjoyed with Liz's dancing. And her mother loved her.

Julie jumped up and down, cheering and shouting words Liz couldn't hear amid the noise. Julie put her fingers to her lips and whistled, causing Liz to erupt in laughter.

Sam clapped enthusiastically and flashed them the thumbs-up. He pulled a hanky from his back pocket and wiped the perspiration from his brow. A man behind Sam patted him on the shoulder and said something that caused Sam to smile broadly, motion toward Tyler, and say "my son." Liz caught Tyler's eyes and watched him break into a huge smile, basking in paternal approval like the prodigal son.

As Liz and Tyler retreated to the back room, the cheering continued until the sounds were silenced by the close of the door. They huffed in exhaustion and sat while the next couple departed for their performance and the other couples milled around anxiously, waiting for the contest to end and the judges to announce the verdict.

"Think we were any good?" asked Tyler, waggling his eyebrows. "Did you hear that crowd? We nailed it, Liz, nailed it." He pumped his arm, then threw Liz a high five.

She smiled, saying nothing.

Tyler grabbed her shoulders and shook them gently. "Good stuff, Liz. We're an awesome dance team. Did you feel it?"

She nodded. "Yes, yes, I did." They'd danced well—fabulously, in fact—but that's not what she'd felt. Talent and many hours of grueling practice might have caused her to move her feet in the right direction on that dance floor, but Tyler's words that prefaced their dance had added the song to her heart and the lilt to her feet. Had he forgotten what he'd said? Or did he remember and regret opening his mouth?

Liz swallowed hard. "Tyler, before we danced, you said . . ."

Her words were interrupted when one of the contest workers, a very short man whose face had the exaggerated expression of a clown's painted on a sideshow wall, opened the door. "Okay, boys and girls. Onto the dance floor for the judging. Good luck, everyone." He continued to smile widely as he held the door and the dancers filed by.

Liz and Tyler were the last to leave the waiting room. Tyler reached for her hand before they stepped onto the floor and gave her a reassuring squeeze. They lined up with the other six couples, squinting in the intense light.

A woman who looked like a cross between a super-model and a Renoir painting carried out a giant check for ten thousand dollars and a large gold trophy adorned with a dancing couple.

"Ladies and gentlemen," the announcer said, approaching the table. "One of these lucky couples will walk away this evening with this beautiful trophy and this even more beautiful ten thousand dollar grand prize." The audience clapped. "All of our couples did a bang up job, but we can have only winner."

The announcer walked to the long dais next to the orchestra, where the three judges sat. One judge handed him an envelope, and he returned to the center of the floor, holding the envelope high in the air.

"The judges have made their decision." He turned so the entire audience could see the envelope, the holy grail of the contest. He faced the contestants. "Dancers, are you ready?"

Liz felt Tyler's grip tighten. She returned it with even more intensity. She glanced at him, barely blinking. She looked at Grace, sitting straighter in her chair, hands folded tightly in her lap, mouth drawn tighter than usual. Liz's eyes then fell on the check. Ten thousand dollars looked even larger than it sounded. That money would change her life right now—if it was possible for it to be transformed even more than had already been done. She looked again at Tyler, who was smiling at her with a warmth that made her want to believe she'd already won the prize. She could live on the exhilaration of this moment for a lifetime.

"Ladies and gentleman," the announcer said, his voice soaked with mystery. He tore open the envelope and withdrew a stiff card. He smiled at the dancers and then at the audience, prolonging the drama of the moment. "The moment we've all been waiting for. The winning couple is . . ."

Chapter Eighteen

"They did more spins, and their steps were more complicated," Liz explained to Tyler. She kicked off her silver heels and watched them skid across the deck of his boat like falling stars in the night sky.

As soon as the contest winner was announced, the hall was lost in a storm of falling confetti, and everyone's attention was focused on the winners; Tyler took Liz by the hand and hurried out the door. He sat her on the back of his motorcycle, told her to hang on tight and wrap her dress around her legs, and took off through town. She had no idea where he was going, and she didn't care. Wherever it was, Tyler had wanted her with him. It was time to let him take the reins. Her energy was zapped, her mind a jumble of problems still to be solved. On her ride down Bridge Street on the back of his motorcycle, her dress billowed behind like a red night cloud, and she had no idea where they were going. But when they arrived at the harbor, she couldn't have thought of a better place to be.

Tyler yanked off his bow tie and threw it down the galley steps. "I still say we were better." He plopped into the seat next to her.

His disappointment delighted Liz. He truly had had his heart set on victory, and he'd practiced as if he had his eye on the prize. She'd wanted to win this contest as much for Tyler as for herself. Liz smiled sweetly, inhaled, and chose her words carefully. "We had more showmanship and polish, better clothes," she said with unbiased analysis, holding up the sash of her dress. "But they threw in some moves that tipped the scales in their favor." She formed fists and shook them. "I should have pushed us harder, added some tougher steps. I was too easy on us, Tyler. That wasn't fair to you."

Tyler inched a little closer. "Do you always have to be so professional, so just? Even though we got a raw deal, you can't even bring yourself to dislike the judges and their crummy contest."

She was offended by his comment. Didn't he realize how wounded she was? How shattered her plans, her life, were? The decision of the judges put a whole new twist on the amazingly wacky life of Liz Pruitt. And brought with it a new mess of worries. But there would be no way for Tyler to understand this. He was just the nice guy who'd agreed to dance with her. Who'd practiced his heart out and outshone every man in that contest with his flair and pizzazz. She'd really sold him short by not pushing him to learn tougher moves she feared would be too difficult for an amateur. She'd intended to do him a favor when, in fact, she had hurt him. Hurt both of them by not taking a chance, not having more guts. The story of her life.

Liz lowered her eyes. She wasn't about to hurt him more by lying. "Tyler, I'd never compromise my passion for dance by giving credit to a couple who didn't deserve the prize. Even if that couple was us. That just wouldn't feel right." She stood and walked to the side of the boat, looking out onto Lake Ontario disguised as a great nothingness in the inky night.

"Then what would feel right?" He approached her from behind and gently turned her to him. She felt the warmth of his breath in the chill of the night air and smelled the citrus bite of his cologne.

"I don't know," Liz said, her eyes misting. "That's what scares me. That dance had all the right feelings for me. If that wasn't enough for us to . . . to win, then I have no other options. If your words weren't . . . weren't meant . . ."

He brushed away a single tear as it glided down her cheek. "My words?"

She pushed by him, wrapping her arms around herself and moving to the other side of the boat, where she had a clear view of the moon glow reflecting on the water with shimmery streaks.

They wallowed in awkward silence for several moments, the clank of the buoy bell the only sound in the vast emptiness.

Tyler neared her. "Uh, Liz," he began, removing the silk handkerchief hanging by only a corner from his pocket. "About those words . . ."

She held up a hand, longing to silence him, stop him from saying the words that would confirm how foolish she'd been to think she and Tyler would ever be anything more than just former acquaintances who'd stumbled upon each other at a mutually convenient time. She'd overstepped her bounds by asking him to dance with her, help her secure a few precious dollars to help save her financially challenged mother. She'd compromised her principles by agreeing to pretend to be his fiancée; then she wasn't even brave enough to admit to herself that deep down she'd hoped the fantasy would become the real thing.

"Don't worry, Tyler. I'll keep my end of the bargain. Just because we lost the contest, I won't leave you high and dry. I'll continue to pretend to be your fiancée." It was the least she could do.

"Uh, yeah, about that . . ." Tyler said, hesitating.

"You don't have to explain." Liz wanted to spare him the indignity of saying more and spare herself from hearing words that would surely shoot another dagger into her aching heart.

He placed his hands on her shoulders, squaring her to him. He placed a finger under her chin and raised her head, forcing her to look into his eyes. "Liz, those words I said before the dance . . . I meant them."

She studied his eyes, those crystal blue spheres, like a fortune-teller looking for answers. "Like a friend, right, Tyler? You said you loved me because we've become friends, right?" She forced her emotions to remain in check.

He smiled, looking softer, warmer than she'd seen before. For all the hours they'd spent in each other's arms dancing, for all the physical closeness they'd shared, she'd never seen Tyler in just the way he looked at this instant. Never felt such elation from being so close to him.

"You *are* my friend, Liz. A very special friend. But that's not why I love you." Each word was a distinct syllable meant to be heard, to be understood.

"So you felt it too. While we were dancing. You had those feelings too, didn't you?"

"I sure did," he said. "Same thing I felt when you dropped two quarters onto my foot and when your dog chased a squirrel by my boat and you jumped over that rock like a gazelle." He smiled widely. "And that night when I first kissed you. What a woman you are, Liz Pruitt!"

Heat surged through Liz, and she longed for the cooling balm of the night air.

"And if I look deep into my heart, I realize I felt it all those years ago when I mooched pens from the quiet little girl sitting behind me in homeroom."

Liz felt her cheeks burn.

He pulled her close, and they embraced, hearts beating in a syncopation not unlike their carefully choreographed dance routine. "I love you, Liz."

Though she could barely take a breath, she managed to return his sentiments. "I love you too, Tyler." Liz raised her head and looked into his eyes. "We've just lost the dance contest, and that means my mother will lose her dance studio. I shouldn't feel like the happiest woman on the planet."

"I've been thinking," he said. "We had some pretty good plans in place to fake out that silly Augustine Trust. I was totally prepared to claim my money from the trust, even under less-than-honorable circumstances, and pay it back when our fake engagement hit the skids. But for the life of me, I had no idea how I was going to surrender you as my fiancée."

He released her and paced across the deck, leaning on the side of the boat, rocking gently with the waves. "My father has been making all these wedding plans and telling his cronies about his son's engagement like it's the social event of the century. And you already have a ring." He pointed to her hand, at the diamond flickering in the moonlight.

Liz caught her breath, and her gut tightened. She shuffled her feet, willing them to stand still, not dance. Not leap into the sky and soar among the stars.

"If we were to . . . to *really* get married, I wouldn't have to pay back the trust, and we could use the money to fix this boat and pay your mother's debts." He looked at her intently. "Of course, there is that stipulation in the trust about providing for the next generation of Augustines, which would mean we'd need to bring some little Augustines into the picture one of these days." He winked devilishly.

Liz started quaking from the inside out.

"It would be a shame for my father to have to tell his buddies there would be no wedding. Seems that for the first time ever, I've done something he's proud of by choosing you for my future wife. He wouldn't take too kindly to my squashing those wedding plans. Augustines like things to go their way. We're used to getting what we want." He crossed his arms and tilted his head toward her, his expression self-assured and determined.

Liz swallowed hard.

"And that ring just looks so magnificent on your hand. Much better than it did sitting in the safe at home."

Liz raised her eyes, waiting for Tyler to continue, to finish the conversation he'd started. She shot him an impish grin.

"You said you owed me two debts of gratitude. You agreed to be my fake fiancée, which was definitely one debt paid. I guess that leaves one more." He walked slowly to her, each step a dramatic movement that could easily have been choreographed into a dance. "Would a fine woman like you ever consider marrying—for real—a guy like me?" He took her hands and raised them to his lips, gently kissing her fingertips.

Tears sprang to her eyes, and joy flooded her soul while she relished each precious sensation. She wanted to scream yes, yes, yes. But she needed to be sure. Maybe the Augustines liked things to go their way, but the Pruitts liked things to be right. "Would you have proposed if we'd won the contest? If our original plans worked out and we'd won the prize?"

"Liz, all the money from that contest would have been worthless if I couldn't have the one prize I really wanted. You. All I've ever wanted was you. So, will the *fake* future Mrs. Tyler Augustine do me the honor of becoming the *real* future Mrs. Tyler Augustine? Will you marry me, Liz?"

She raised her arms in a dance pose, shoulders straight, elbows extended, and placed them around his shoulders. "Let's try this one more time," she said. "We should have won that contest. I know we can do it. Let's try again. Ready? One, two, three . . ."

"Together," they said in unison.

They took a few spins around the deck, bathed in the ebony night, smiles illuminated by the starlit sky and the glow from their souls.

"We're especially good on the 'together' part," Liz said softly. "Promise me you'll dance just like that at our wedding reception," she added, raising a hand and placing it gently on his cheek. "The *real* Mrs. Tyler Augustine would love to dance with her *real* husband."

ML

5/12